"I can't do a job if I'm being sabotaged…"

"Do you feel he is trying to get you to quit?"

Tracey swallowed the rest of her coffee. "I honestly don't know, Roce, but my instincts are telling me yes."

"Mine are saying the same thing. He needs watching, Tracey. Be careful."

"I will. Tomorrow I'll just play 'I Spy' games with the children on whatever trail we take. There'll be nothing for him to criticize."

"He's picked the wrong woman to drive away. You're a warrior."

Their eyes held. "I'll take that as a compliment."

"Wish I could ride with you. I already know the prize I want," he said with a half smile that sent a thrill racing through her body.

So do I.

Funny how a simple dinner had suddenly made her so breathless.

Dear Reader,

This third book in the Sapphire Mountain Cowboys series has been so enjoyable to write. A cowboy who loves and cares about animals is rather special to me. While I was writing this novel, I remembered something that happened to my daughter's beloved white bichon frise, Beauty.

I was at my daughter's house making chocolate-chip cookies for my grandchildren. The pan I'd gotten out of the cupboard happened to nudge the bag of chocolate chips off the island counter to the floor on the other side. I hurried around to pick it up, but Beauty had gotten to it first and dragged it to another part of the kitchen to eat the contents before I could reach her. I was horrified and immediately drove her to the vet, whose hospital is at the end of Salt Lake Valley near the Oquirrh Mountains. He had horses in the pasture behind his office and was a cowboy with a lot of charm. Within minutes he'd pumped Beauty's stomach, saving her! I've never been so grateful in my life.

I'm quite sure he's the person I was thinking of when I decided to write Dr. Roce Clayton's story. Roce is one of those marvelous Montana Clayton brothers—four heroes who are all adored by the women who come into their lives.

Enjoy!

Rebecca Winters

COWBOY DOCTOR

REBECCA WINTERS

HARLEQUIN® WESTERN ROMANCE

Recycling programs
for this product may
not exist in your area.

ISBN-13: 978-0-373-75770-1

Cowboy Doctor

Rebecca Winters, whose family of four children has now swelled to include five beautiful grandchildren, lives in Salt Lake City, Utah, in the land of the Rocky Mountains. Living near canyons and high alpine meadows full of wildflowers, she never runs out of places to explore. They, plus her favorite vacation spots in Europe, often end up as backgrounds for her romance novels, because writing is her passion, along with her family and church.

Rebecca loves to hear from readers. If you wish to email her, please visit her website, cleanromances.com.

Books by Rebecca Winters

Harlequin Western Romance

Sapphire Mountain Cowboys

A Valentine for the Cowboy
Made for the Rancher

Lone Star Lawmen

The Texas Ranger's Bride
The Texas Ranger's Nanny
The Texas Ranger's Family
Her Texas Ranger Hero

Hitting Rocks Cowboys

In a Cowboy's Arms
A Cowboy's Heart
The New Cowboy
A Montana Cowboy

Visit the Author Profile page
at Harlequin.com for more titles.

To James Alfred "Alf" Wight, better known by the pen name James Herriot. He was a British veterinary surgeon and writer who used his many years of experience to write a series of books, each consisting of stories about animals and their owners. He's best known for his semiautobiographical works beginning with *All Creatures Great and Small*. In 1972 a British television series was adapted from the books, also titled *All Creatures Great and Small*. Thanks to him, I was given hours and hours of sheer pleasure and developed an even greater appreciation of all God's creatures.

Chapter One

"Last on the program is Dr. Rocelin Clayton, who worked closely with Hannah for the last three years, right up to her death."

Pastor McKinney nodded to Roce, who walked to the lectern.

The Presbyterian church on Spruce Street was filled to overflowing. People from all over had come to pay their respects to the eighty-three-year-old veterinarian who'd practiced here in Missoula, Montana, for over fifty years.

Roce stood before the audience, some of whom he'd helped after Hannah had taken him into her practice. This was a sad day for him. The only other time he'd ever spoken at a funeral was at his father's, almost two years ago. He was forced to clear his throat several times before speaking.

"A paragon has left us, and no one is more bereaved than I am. Dr. Hannah Larabee, owner of the Larabee Veterinarian Hospital, was not only a legend in these parts, she was the best boss a man could have hoped to work for right out of veterinary school.

"I didn't get the opportunity to meet her beloved Tom, her veterinarian husband who started the hospital with her. He died two years before I was hired. Hannah's sudden fatal heart attack is proof that she gave her all to the animals big and small that God put on this earth for our comfort and enjoyment.

"Not long ago she told me that she never met an animal she didn't like, and that when she got to heaven, she planned to visit every one of those creatures who'd already passed on."

His eyes smarted.

"I bet that right now they're all standing in line to see her again. It's possible that, at this very moment, she's talking to them in her loving voice, commiserating with them about the ailments they'd suffered on earth."

He heard gentle laughter from the audience and saw a lot of people wiping their eyes. The church was filled with animal lovers from western Montana who knew exactly what he was talking about.

"We're all going to miss her and the great blessing she was to this community. Her family has to be so proud of what she accomplished on this earth.

"If we were all as good as Hannah, what a beautiful world this would be."

When he took his seat, the pastor stood before them once more. "We'll now sing our parting hymn—it was known to be Hannah's favorite—'Dear to the Heart of the Shepherd.'"

During the singing, one line stood out to Roce:

"Dear are the sheep of His fold." That sounded like Hannah.

After the prayer, everyone followed the funeral procession to the cemetery. Roce rode with his mother and Toly. His youngest brother had a rodeo to get back to in Omaha and was in town for only a few more hours. His other two brothers, Eli and Wymon, trailed them in their cars with their wives. Hannah had touched all their lives.

Roce hadn't felt this lost since his father had died. With Hannah's death, the time had come for him to go his own way and make decisions, whether he wanted to or not. This was a day he hadn't thought would come for several more years. If Roce didn't buy the veterinary hospital and take over, Hannah's family would put it up for sale and someone else would be in charge. They might not want to keep Roce on. In order for him to buy the practice, he would have to take out a big loan.

But in his heart, his secret hope had been to open his own hospital on the Clayton Cattle Ranch outside Stevensville, Montana. Besides serving as vet to the ranch, as well as the people in Ravalli County, he could help out his mom and brothers with ranching activities. To do that, he would have to discuss it with the family, and he didn't know how they would feel.

Even if it were possible, he had to consider that moving to the ranch would mean he'd lose clients who lived in Missoula, a half hour away. To start a new practice on the ranch would take time. And there was the question of where to build a new structure that wouldn't impose on the family.

Whatever happened, he would have to put his small condo in Missoula up for sale. The location near the hospital had made life easier when there'd been emergencies that had called him out in the middle of the night. It wasn't fully paid for, but he needed as much money as he could put together no matter what direction he chose to go. All these thoughts bombarded him as they drove away from the cemetery.

Later, after they'd dropped Toly off at the airport and he was alone with his mom on the drive back to the ranch, she turned to him and said, "Roce—your talk had everyone in tears. I'm so proud to be your mother. But now that we're alone, I can tell there's something serious on your mind, so let's talk about it."

He smiled. "What do you think you know?"

"That you've come to a fork in the road. Your dad hoped you'd become our ranch veterinarian. When the time came, he had a spot all picked out for you."

Roce's hands tightened on the steering wheel. This was the first he'd heard about it. "What area would that be?"

"The old sheep station house."

His thoughts reeled. "The bungalow right off the highway?" Long ago there'd been no road there, only trampled ground from bringing through the sheep.

She nodded. "When they built the highway, the house was boarded up, and blocked off by the fencing."

"Why didn't Dad do something with it?"

"He wanted all our homes and outbuildings to be

centered together, higher on the mountain. But when you became a vet, he told me he hoped to make renovations on the station so you could open up your practice on our property. As you can see, it would be the perfect place for a hospital, with easy access to the highway. Let's take a look at it."

Roce was in shock. He'd almost forgotten it was there. A bank of trees camouflaged most of it. At her urging he drove past the entrance to the ranch and on to the boundary of their property. After parking on the highway shoulder, he got out with his mom and walked over to the fence.

Roce rested his arms on top and took a good, long look at the one-story log house they could see through the leaves. His mother stood next to him. "All you'd have to do is remove part of this fencing and a few trees. Then a new road into the parking area could be constructed, with a sign that says Clayton Veterinary Hospital."

While his mother kept talking, Roce's heartbeat began to pick up speed.

"Besides equipping a new surgery, you'd have to put in new plumbing, and the building needs new paint. Your brothers and I have been talking. With their help, you could be in business in no time."

He cleared his throat. "I couldn't ask them to do that."

But all the time she was talking, he could see adding an office next to the surgery. He would have to install electronic locks for the front and back doors because of the drugs he would have to keep on the premises.

"Your family has volunteered, Roce. Remember when you helped Wymon build a second story on his house? Now they want to pitch in for you on a second story. A bedroom and bathroom upstairs? I'm thinking you could live here a long time, and still keep your horse in the barn with ours. And at a future date, you may want to build your own ranch house for the family you'll have one day."

After all these years his mom was still holding out that he'd find the right woman for him, but Roce feared the woman of his dreams didn't exist. He hated to shatter his mom's hopes of that happening, though, especially when she'd just offered this gift out of the blue. So many emotions overwhelmed him. He pulled his mother into his arms and gave her a long hug.

Two months later

THE SATURDAY DRIVE from Polson to Hamilton, Montana, turned out to be beautiful. It was June 2, and the warm weather had arrived in Bitterroot Valley. Tracey Marcroft opened the window of her white Honda, drawing in a deep breath of pine-scented air.

As she took in the vision before her, she didn't care that the breeze tangled her hair. After the last nine months, she was finally free from the responsibilities of teaching school, and was looking forward to her summer job at the Rocky Point Dude Ranch. She loved her sixth graders, but couldn't wait to work with families who'd come out here on vacation to horseback ride, another one of her passions.

During spring break, she'd interviewed with John Hunter, a man who'd made it big in oil and owned the dude ranch. The patriarch of his large family had been a close friend of her grandpa Ben's before moving from Polson. He'd been the one to show her the facilities and he'd made her feel very welcome. The stories he'd told about him and her grandfather in their younger years riding around Flathead country had fascinated her.

She liked John and his wife, Sylvia, a lot, and was thrilled when they offered her the job, along with her own little cabin. Besides the fact that John praised her for the way she rode and handled the horses during their ride, he'd seemed especially pleased to hear that she taught school and understood kids. They had plenty of families with younger children who could benefit from her expertise.

Tracey was indebted to her grandfather for suggesting she get in touch with John for the job. She'd always been close to her grandpa, who'd been living with her family for the last two years since her grandmother had died. Tracey wanted to be an asset to the dude ranch and make him proud. Hopefully, three months out here in a different part of Montana would give her a new lease on life.

A year ago this past Christmas, she'd expected her boyfriend, Jeff Atkins, to return from his deployment overseas so they could plan their wedding. They'd met in college at the University of Montana in Missoula.

But he'd been killed in an ambush, along with two other men in his platoon. Since then, she'd been trying to get over the pain. Her parents and her older brother,

Max, had done what they could to comfort her. But time had to do the rest.

It was two in the afternoon when she reached Stevensville. She felt hunger pains and pulled into a drive-through behind a line of tourists to grab a hamburger and a soda.

While she waited, she phoned her best friend, Barb, who was married and worked as a paralegal in Polson. Tracey hadn't had a chance to say goodbye to her. During their talk, Barb promised that she and her husband would come visit over the July Fourth holiday. Pleased that she'd be seeing her friend next month, Tracey hung up after getting her meal.

She drove out to the highway again for the last twenty-minute leg of her trip. While munching on her fries, Tracey rounded the long curve in the road, marveling at the sight of the magnificent Sapphire Mountains flanking the valley. In her mind's eye, they were filled with heaps of dazzling blue gemstones. When she'd been a child, that image had delighted her imagination. It still did.

A little farther on she saw a sign for Clayton Veterinary Hospital, and slowed down while she finished off her fries. Funny that she hadn't seen it in the spring, when she'd first driven this way. To her recollection, there'd been a bank of trees all along the highway.

Set against a backdrop of pines was a small, yet charming log cabin. There weren't any cars in the parking lot, but she glimpsed a horse trailer at the side of the house before she sped up.

The setup reminded her of Laura Ingalls Wilder's

book *Little House in the Big Woods*, one of Tracey's favorites in the series. She'd always been an avid reader. Throughout her young years she'd imagined herself as Laura, riding around on her own horse.

Tracey had gone through several horses in her life, her current one being Spirit, her gelding, who was getting very old and needed regular checkups with her family's vet in Kalispell. Her mom and dad were taking care of him while she was gone this summer.

When she reached Hamilton, she took a left. She'd learned that the Hunter family lived in their own homes in town when they weren't on duty at the ranch. It was only a two-mile commute to the dude ranch sitting on five hundred acres of prime land.

The large foyer with its office and check-in counter divided the big Western ranch house into two parts. One side contained the common areas, consisting of an activity room, dining room and kitchen, plus a great room with a fireplace that rose to the vaulted ceiling. The other side had been remodeled into bedrooms to house forty people at a time.

Tennis courts and a swimming pool with a cabana had been built at the side of the ranch house. The stable, barn and corral lay behind the whole facility. To the side of the corral were a dozen small cabins for the summer staff.

There were sheds housing fishing gear, white-water rafts—everything the vacationer could ask for. As John had explained, the Bitterroot River offered rafters and floaters a trip down one of the most scenic waterways in Montana, traveling through the Bitterroot and Sapphire mountains. From those vantage points, the view of the wide, lush valley was unforgettable.

The ideal setup appealed to Tracy, who pulled up in front of the ranch house to let John know she'd arrived. It wouldn't be open for summer vacationers until the day after tomorrow. That gave her time to get more acquainted with the facilities, particularly the horses.

She got out of the car and walked inside. A cute brunette woman in her early twenties was manning the front desk. She broke out in a smile when she saw her approach.

"You have to be Tracey Marcroft."

"Yes."

"I'm Fran Hunter. I'm married to Wes, who's John's grandson. At breakfast he said you'd be coming today. He told me and Wes, and I quote, 'She's the most beautiful young woman you ever saw, and she can ride a horse like nobody's business!'"

Tracey chuckled. It was hard to know what to say after that. "He sounds as full of it as my grandpa Ben, but thank you. I've been looking forward to meeting the rest of your family."

"We're a big one."

"So I've gathered. I'll try to learn names fast."

"Don't worry about it. Granddad is waiting for you in his office. Just come around behind the counter."

Pleased that she acted so friendly, Tracy did her bidding. The door at the end of the hallway had been left open. She saw John seated at his desk. He was on the phone but waved at her to come on in.

A lean, lanky man with a ton of energy, he had a

wonderful head of salt-and-pepper hair. "Welcome, my dear," he said, after hanging up the phone. "Sylvia and I are thrilled you've joined us." He came around to give her a hug.

"I'm the one who's excited. Grandpa Ben sends his love with this." She put a brightly wrapped box on his desk. "He said it's chocolate-covered cashews."

"My favorite. He remembered. Thank you." His eyes twinkled. "I plan to give him a call later and let him know you arrived. For the rest of today and tomorrow, I want you to get more acquainted with the place and staff. Fran, Wes's wife, is a sweetheart and runs the front desk most of the time. She'll take care of you. Go for a swim, visit the barn and stable. Do whatever you want."

"Thank you."

"My son Sheldon and his wife Janet organize the trail rides with the forest service and are in charge of procuring our horses. Among them we have six ponies for our littlest riders."

"Oh—I can't wait to see them!"

"They're a hit with everyone. My grandson, Wes, Sheldon and Janet's son, runs the stable. I've told Wes to let you pick out the horse you'd like to ride while you're here this summer."

"I can't wait. Just so you know, I've brought my own saddle and gear."

"Wonderful. Fran will give you the key to your cabin. It's number two. My wife and I will see you at dinner at seven."

"I'd love that."

When she went back to the counter, Fran introduced her to another of John's sons named Thad. You couldn't mistake him for anyone else. He had the same lanky look as his dad. "Uncle Thad is head of security. He deals with any emergencies or illness situations, and maintains all our equipment and cabins."

Tracey shook his hand. "It's so nice to meet you."

"We're glad to have you on board. If you have any concerns, come see me."

"I will."

"See you at dinner."

After he walked away, Fran said, "Later on I'll introduce you to everyone else. Uncle Thad's wife, Noreen, is head of housekeeping and laundry. You'll also meet my grandma Sylvia and my aunt Deanna. They're in charge of food and run the kitchen. Deanna's husband, my uncle Paul, oversees all the other activities like fishing and river rafting."

"I'm afraid my head is spinning with so many names."

"There are more. Along with Wes, you'll be doing trail rides with Colette, who's married to Rod. He's Uncle Paul and Deanna's son. But you'll figure it all out soon enough."

"I understand you all live in town."

"Yes, but we have a rotation system so we have plenty of staff on duty 24/7."

"That's good to know."

"Let me assure you we're close enough to the ranch to be here on a moment's notice if necessary. Wes's grandfather made it possible for Wes and me to get into a small house after we were first married. I had imagined we'd be living in an apartment for several years, so we're very lucky."

"My grandfather sings his praises. I think that's wonderful." Tracey and Jeff would have moved to an apartment first, but it didn't happen, and she needed to stop living in the past. That's why she'd wanted this new job here for the summer.

"Wes's parents are so generous, too, and have made everything great for us. I've married into the best family in the world. But that's enough talking about me. I hear you're an elementary school teacher. I admire you for being able to handle a roomful of children all day long."

"It's a challenge, but I love it."

"Do you have a boyfriend back home who's going to miss you?"

Tracey's eyes smarted. "I was engaged to be married, but my fiancé was killed while serving in the military. I'm still trying to get over it."

A hand went to Fran's throat. "I didn't know. I'm sorry to have gone on and on about me and Wes."

"Don't you worry about anything. It happened eighteen months ago and I'm doing much better."

"I'm glad to hear that. If you ever want to talk, I'm available. I met Wes at junior college. We dated and I fell in love with him. But there were several long periods when he didn't call me. Both times I thought it was over and could hardly bear it. I remember those times, and I'm so sorry for your loss."

"Don't say another word. I'm just happy you two got back together."

"It was like a miracle. One day he showed up at my dorm and we ended up getting married. But I'm keeping you from getting settled, so I'll drive with you to your cabin. It's number two."

"Thank you." Fran was a very compassionate person. Tracey liked her. They left the ranch house and got in her car. She started the engine and, following Fran's directions, drove them past a corral holding half a dozen horses to the log cabins in the distance.

Only then did it dawn on Tracey how lucky she was to be working for the Hunter family. It made her realize how much John Hunter must revere her grandpa, letting her come work for them as he had. She would do everything she could to fit in, and Fran was already making it easy.

She pulled up in front of her designated cabin. Fran got out and opened the door while Tracey carried in her luggage. The first thing she saw in the little living-room-slash-kitchen was a yellow vase filled with white daisies placed on the round dinette table. A card peeked out of it. She put down her bags and opened the envelope.

"Welcome to the Rocky Point Dude Ranch. I hope the experience here will help mend your broken heart. —John."

Hot tears burned her eyelids. Tracey didn't know her grandfather had confided in John about Jeff. She was so touched she could hardly talk.

"How lovely." Her voice faltered.

"Granddad says you're the very special grand-daughter of his oldest, best friend."

Tracey turned around. "I can't thank all of you enough for your kindness."

"It's a pleasure. Can I do anything else for you?"

"I'll be fine. Do you want me to drive you back?"

"Oh, no. I need the walk. We'll see you in the dining room at seven for a special dinner to kick off the summer season. And remember, come on over to the ranch house anytime if you need someone to talk to. I know there are times when I do." Fran put the front door key on the table before leaving.

That sounded like a lonely statement to Tracey.

While mulling it over, she walked into the bedroom with its two twin beds, dressers and closet. The other door of the main room led to the bathroom. She liked the blue-green-and-white-plaid decor of the cabin.

A painting of the Sapphire Mountains hung on the log wall over the small couch. With a mini fridge, microwave, TV and internet, she would be perfectly happy here.

The first thing she did was sit down at the table and call her parents. Most of all she wanted to thank her grandpa and tell him about the daisies John had left for her. After a tearful conversation with him while she expressed her gratitude, Tracey freshened up and drove her car over to the barn to unload her saddle and gear.

A sandy-haired guy who looked to be college age caught sight of her. "Hey—need help?" He walked up to her with a smile you couldn't miss. "I'm Grady Cox."

"Hi, Grady. I'm Tracey Marcroft and will be helping on the trail rides. If you could show me the tack room?"

"Let me carry your saddle."

"Thank you." She brought the rest of the gear and followed him through the long barn to the end room. "Were you hired for the summer?"

"That's right. I'm a student at Montana State. This will be my third year working with the horses. Occasionally I help on the trail rides, too. Are you from around here? In college?"

She chuckled. He worked fast. "I graduated from the University of Montana two years ago and teach elementary school in Polson."

He shook his head. "I never remember having a schoolteacher who looked like you. This has to be my lucky day."

She smiled, but she wasn't attracted to him, and put her gear away, not wanting to give him any encouragement by responding. "Mr. Hunter told me Wes is in charge of the stable. Is he on duty? I need to pick out a horse I can ride while I'm here."

"I'll help you do that while he's gone."

"Will it be all right?"

"That's my job. Do you have a preference?"

"Not really. I'm sure Mr. Hunter wouldn't have anything but the best horses."

"You're right about that. Why don't we walk to the corral? Any one of the quarter horses out there would be a great choice for you. I've been exercising them. Of course, we have more here in the barn if you want to look them over, too."

"Thank you."

She was glad he had other things to do and left her alone in the corral. For the next hour, Tracey examined each horse and walked it around. She took her measure of the three mares: a sorrel, a black and a bay. The three other horses were geldings, all of them buckskins.

When she'd finished, she walked into the barn to look over the other horses before she made a decision. When she came to the dun gelding, she knew the splendid horse was the one she wanted, and Tracey walked him out of his stall to the corral.

But as she was leading him around, she noticed his right front leg was limping a little. That wasn't good. She lifted his hoof to inspect it. When she applied pressure to the sole, the horse let out a distressed grunt.

"You poor thing." She patted his neck to settle him before calling to Grady, who'd gone out to the corral. "Come and look. This horse is in pain."

He walked over with a frown. "That's Wes's horse."

"Oh! I thought all the horses were available."

"Sorry. Not Chief. I should have said something. He's off-limits."

"Still, he's limping and needs attention."

"I've never noticed him do that before. Are you sure?"

"Positive."

"You'd better take him back to the stall. I'll talk to Wes about it as soon as he shows up. He went to town several hours ago."

"I'm afraid something should be done soon," she

said, as she slowly walked him back inside. "Chief needs a vet, don't you, boy?" She hugged his neck.

Grady watched her, looking uncertain and upset. "I'm sure you're right."

"Tell you what. I'm going back to the ranch house now to talk to John about this."

"Maybe you should wait for Wes."

Why did he seem so hesitant? "What if he can't get back right away? The horse needs help. John will know what to do."

Surely Grady Cox didn't want to see the horse suffer. You needed to be proactive to keep animals safe and healthy. She'd learned the same thing working with children. When something went wrong, you didn't wait. "Thanks for your help, Grady. See you later."

"For sure. I assume you're staying in one of the cabins for the summer, too." His eyes played over her with the kind of male interest she didn't want. Since they'd be forced to work together over the summer, she needed to establish a boundary now.

"Yes. I've already settled in."

Without hesitation, she hurried to her car and drove to the ranch house. When she walked in, no one was at the front desk. Tracey took the initiative and walked around the counter to John's office. To her frustration, he wasn't there, either.

She went back outside to her car. Dinner wouldn't be for another hour. The only thing to do was return to her cabin and change. Because they were having a special welcome dinner, she decided to wear her denim skirt and a Western blouse with snaps.

Though she couldn't bear to see an animal in pain, she had no choice but to wait until then. Hopefully, Wes might have returned and Grady would have already told him about Chief. By now she hoped their vet would have been called.

At five to seven she drove back to the ranch house, where the family had started to gather in the big dining room. She spotted John behind the counter and rushed over to talk to him.

He gave her a big smile. "Have you had a good afternoon?"

"It's been terrific, but I'm worried about one of your horses." She told him what she'd discovered. "Wes wasn't there, but I pointed out the problem to Grady."

His brows met. "Grady didn't know he was limping?"

"No. He seemed surprised."

"Well, you're absolutely right. Chief needs a vet, but I don't know that much about the one we've just inherited. Our old vet passed away recently. Still, I'll call him now. Come in the office with me before we have dinner."

Tracey followed him down the hall, gratified because he recognized the emergency situation and would take care of it. She sat down and listened while he looked up the number on his computer and made the phone call.

In a minute he hung up and shook his head. "Dr. Cruz isn't available until Monday."

"Does he practice here in Hamilton?"

"No. Darby. It's only fifteen miles away, but I'm

going to have to find someone else. There's a good vet in Anaconda."

"Isn't that kind of far from here?"

"Yes, but I have to start somewhere."

While he searched on the computer, she suddenly remembered something.

"John? On my way to Hamilton I passed a sign that said Clayton Veterinary Hospital. It's right off the highway about fifteen minutes from here. Have you ever heard of it?"

He blinked. "I didn't know it existed. You're sure about that?"

"Yes. I slowed down because I didn't remember seeing it when I came here for the interview in the spring. It has to be brand-new."

"That's very interesting. If that vet is a Clayton, then it's probably their ranch's vet who handles large animals."

"What ranch is that?"

"The Clayton Cattle Ranch. They're well-known around these parts. It's worth a call to see if someone there can check out Chief this evening. He's too valuable a horse to lose."

John called information and before long she heard him talking to someone else. John outlined the situation before he handed her the phone. "Dr. Clayton wants you to tell him what you saw."

With her heart pounding, she took it from him. "Hello? Dr. Clayton? This is Tracy Marcroft. I was out in the barn earlier. As I led Chief out to the corral,

I noticed he was limping. I lifted his hoof and the second I touched the sole, he grunted in pain."

"That sounds like it could be a solar abscess, a serious infection that can lead to acute or severe lameness," he replied, in a deep male voice she felt resonate through her system. "Did you notice anything else?"

"No. At first I thought it might be something wrong with the shoe, but that wasn't it."

"Anything more you can think of?"

"His demeanor wasn't normal. His ears weren't up and he wouldn't look at me."

"Excellent observations. If that hoof can be healed in time, the horse owes its life to your quick thinking." For no good reason his compliment caused a tingly sensation to sweep through her. "Let me talk to Mr. Hunter again."

"Of course."

She handed the phone to John. They talked a few more minutes and he gave the other man directions to the dude ranch before hanging up. "The doctor will be here in an hour." He squeezed her hand. "Bless you for catching this, Tracey. Let's hurry in to dinner, and then we'll meet him at the barn."

Chapter Two

Roce hung up the phone and wheeled around on his stool. "Our first new patient, Daisy! Who would have thought it would happen on a Saturday night? It has to be some kind of miracle."

He tossed the border collie–Lab mix a treat. Roce had inherited her from Hannah, whose family didn't want the dog she'd adopted. After the funeral, Daisy had kept looking for her. It had torn his heart out and he'd decided to keep her for himself.

When he'd moved to the ranch, he'd brought her with him and they'd become fast friends. His whole family loved the dog, especially his brother Eli's little girl, Libby. She was the daughter from his first marriage, before he'd married his present wife, Brianna.

Libby had regular visitation with her birth mother in town, but when she lived with Eli and Brianna on the ranch, she begged for her uncle Roce to bring his dog to the house.

After first leaving Missoula, Roce had stayed at the main ranch house with his mom. Libby came over all the time to play with Daisy. But when Roce moved into the renovated house down by the highway two months later, she'd wept buckets. He told her she could come to see Daisy anytime she wanted, but she couldn't be consoled.

Once he'd made himself a peanut butter and jelly sandwich, he pulled on a navy long-sleeved hoodie over his jeans. After finding his doctor bag, he made certain he had all the necessary supplies, including Epsom salts and plenty of bandages.

Daisy made whimpering sounds because she knew he was going to leave. He tossed her another treat. "I'll be back later." He could hear her bark as he left the house and got in his dark red, four-door pickup truck.

Twenty minutes later, he turned onto the road leading up to the Rocky Point Dude Ranch. An impressive spread filled his vision. He wound around toward the barn he could see in the distance. As he pulled up to the entrance, he saw an older man and a woman with a knockout figure and long legs waiting for him.

Roce had gone through more attractive women in his life than he cared to admit. Maybe something was wrong with him that he hadn't experienced that affair of the heart like his married brothers. But one thing was certain: when he jumped down from the cab and approached them, he knew that Tracey Marcroft was the most gorgeous woman he'd ever seen in his life.

In the fading light, her shoulder-length blond hair had a metallic sheen to it. Not silver, not gold, but something in between. Her eyes gleamed the lavender-blue color of larkspurs, flowers that grew in the meadows on the Clayton ranch. For a moment, his breath caught at the heavenly sight.

"Dr. Clayton." The older man in the Stetson stepped forward and shook his hand. "I can't thank you enough for coming. Wymon's your brother, right?"

"Yes."

"My son Sheldon and I met him at the rodeo last year."

"Wymon's head of the ranch now."

"It's a small world." He shook his head. "Dr. Cruz, the veterinarian I've been using since our old one died, wasn't available, so I took a chance on you."

"Thank you for calling me. I'm pleased to be of help, Mr. Hunter."

"I have Tracey here to thank for finding you. She just arrived for work today and happened to pass by your hospital on the way."

Her gaze flicked to Roce. "It surprised me. I didn't remember seeing it when I was here in the spring," she explained.

"You wouldn't have. I just set up my practice on the ranch last week, after moving from the hospital in Missoula." He glanced at Mr. Hunter. "Why don't you show me the horse so we can get him out of his pain?"

"Chief is in the third stall."

As he followed the two of them inside the lighted barn, he found it impossible to keep his eyes off Tracey, and the way she moved wearing those cowboy boots.

Mr. Hunter showed him to the stall that housed the dun-colored animal. Roce lowered his bag and approached it. "Chief is a fine-looking quarter horse. They make ideal family horses, don't they?"

"You're right about that."

Roce ran his hand gently over his back and down his right leg. "It's all right, Chief." He moved around in front of him. "Let's take a look at that sore hoof."

When he lifted it, the horse grunted, just as Tracey had said. By the way he held his body, Roce could tell he was in a serious amount of pain. His lower lip had gone tense and he didn't blink. He was too uncomfortable.

With a little probing, Roce found the offending object. "This horse has a hot nail embedded in the wall. I have to get it out. If I could fill a bucket with warm water…and I'll need my bag."

"I'll fill one," Mr. Hunter declared.

"Here's your bag." Tracey brought it to him and knelt to open it. When she looked up, their eyes held. That's when a wave of emotion foreign to anything he'd ever known swept through Roce's body, with such power he was left shaken by the impact.

It was a miracle that he could concentrate on what he was doing while this beautiful woman, who smelled divine, stayed at his side and anticipated his needs.

He removed the nail, releasing the pus. It took a good hour to flush out the wound and soak the hoof in Epsom salts and water. Finally, Roce was able to wrap Chief's foot.

"Do you think he'll be all right?"

Their gazes fused. "That's hard to tell at this point.

He's less tense since the pressure was relieved. I'm going to start him on medication."

Reaching inside his bag, he drew out the balling gun with the antibiotic and placed it in the corner of Chief's mouth. Very gently, he pushed the tip to the back of his tongue. He dispensed the tablet with the plunger and lifted Chief's head to make certain he swallowed it.

"There you go, buddy. We're going to get you better."

"We are," Tracey cooed, with her arms around his neck. "You poor darling."

This woman was a true horse lover. In the background he heard voices. "What's going on, Granddad?" Another male had joined Mr. Hunter.

"I phoned Dr. Clayton to take care of Chief's hoof. It had a hot nail in it."

"Since when? He was fine this morning." The dark-haired younger man, probably in his midtwenties, sounded upset—as he ought to be, considering the pain the horse was in.

"Since Tracey Marcroft arrived this afternoon and noticed he was limping. We have her to thank for saving Chief from going lame, if it's not too late. This is the first time you've had a chance to meet her, isn't it? Tracey? This is my grandson, Wes. You've already met his wife, Fran."

"I did. She's darling. It's nice to meet you, Wes."

He nodded. "Welcome to the ranch." In the next breath he eyed his grandfather. "Where's Dr. Cruz?"

Wes's behavior struck Roce as rude. The man exuded no warmth and hadn't even acknowledged Ms.

Marcroft's contribution. The fact that he completely ignored Roce didn't matter.

"I'm afraid he wasn't available, Wes. You have no idea how fortunate we are that Dr. Clayton was on call and willing to come at a moment's notice."

Wes stood next to his grandfather, but made no comment as Roce put the things back in his bag and moved out of the stall. He addressed the older man. "I'll come every day to soak his hoof until he gets rid of the infection. He'll need a fresh poultice each visit. In ten days to two weeks we'll know if he's back to normal."

"I'm indebted to you." They shook hands. "Allow me to introduce my grandson, Wes, who's in charge of the stable."

"How do you do, Wes?"

The young man made a sound of acknowledgment, but lacked the older man's good manners and didn't extend a hand, prompting Mr. Hunter to speak up. "You'll be seeing Wes when you come again tomorrow."

"Very good."

Roce looked around and saw Tracey Marcroft, who stood a little distance away.

She smiled at him. "I'm so glad you came when you did, Dr. Clayton. Chief seems more at peace already."

"I agree. Getting that nail out did the trick. No animal should have to stay in pain." He turned to Mr. Hunter. "I'll say good-night."

"Come to my office tomorrow after your visit and we'll talk more, Dr. Clayton."

"I'll do that."

Since the arrival of the grandson, the atmosphere had grown chilly.

Much as he would have liked to stay near the horse to observe him awhile longer, and talk to Ms. Marcroft alone for a few minutes, he realized now wasn't the time. But he intended to seek her out tomorrow when he came again. On that happy note, he walked out to the truck and took off.

When he reached his house twenty minutes later and opened the door, Daisy launched herself at him. He let out a deep laugh. Life suddenly looked exciting in ways he couldn't have imagined when he'd left several hours ago.

TRACEY TOOK A shower and got ready for bed, but knew she wouldn't be going to sleep for a while. She was too angry at Wes Hunter, for a variety of reasons. She couldn't comprehend him treating his grandfather like that, and he'd come close to ignoring her and Dr. Clayton. What in heaven's name had been wrong with him?

Before driving to her cabin, she'd noticed John talking to his grandson in private after Dr. Clayton had left in his truck. The older man had shaken his head several times, indicating that they were having an intense conversation. If Wes was upset because he hadn't seen Chief's limp, it didn't warrant his rudeness toward all of them.

No one knew how long the nail had been embedded, but for some reason the infection had started hurting the horse that afternoon. Since she had to work with Wes and it was his horse, she had to hope he wouldn't hold it against her for noticing the problem first. In a normal situation, the number one priority would be to get Chief back to perfect health. She couldn't understand why Wes would be angry that Dr. Clayton had taken care of Chief in a crisis. None of it made sense to her.

But that wasn't all that was bothering her.

When she'd watched the red pickup disappear, she'd wished the dark blond doctor wouldn't have left so fast. The tall, hard-muscled veterinarian was incredibly handsome. Her reaction to him had shocked her. After losing Jeff, she'd thought her heart had died and would never come back to life. But something had gone on this evening when they'd glanced at each other, something she couldn't explain.

It wasn't just his good looks or the intelligence shining in those hazel eyes that appealed to her. He'd displayed a natural affinity for the horse. There was a quiet authority and assurance he possessed that had gentled Chief enough for him to operate on the animal. He was a man in touch with nature, a trait that ranked high with her.

The doctor didn't wear a wedding ring. But maybe because he worked with his hands so much, he left it at home when he went out on calls. If he was married, she'd be a fool to give him another thought.

How uncanny was it that she'd noticed Dr. Clayton's hospital while she'd been driving to the ranch? What were the chances of John calling him in desperation when he couldn't reach his regular vet?

Surprised by her thoughts, after she'd felt dead inside for so long, she grabbed a quilt and made herself comfortable on the couch to watch TV.

At some point she must have fallen asleep, for the next thing she knew someone was knocking on her cabin door. And the sun was streaming in the window above the kitchen sink. Tracey sat up and looked at her watch. Eight-thirty. The knock sounded again.

"Who is it?" she called out.

"Grady Cox."

Tracey silently groaned. He had to be at least three years younger than she.

"They're serving Sunday brunch for all the employees this morning. Do you want to eat with me?"

No, but she couldn't be rude to him. They'd be working together for the next three months. Thank goodness the cabins weren't equipped with phones and he didn't have her cell number. Only John and Fran had access to that information if they needed to get hold of her.

"I'm afraid I'm not up yet. No doubt we'll be seeing each other at some point soon."

"You can count on it. My cabin is number five. The one with the silver Chevy Malibu in front."

"Got it."

When he walked away, Tracey let out a sound of relief and hurried to get ready in jeans and a yellow pullover. Her priority this morning was to check on Chief. She'd planned to skip breakfast, and reached for the granola bar from her purse to eat later on.

After brushing her hair, she put on fresh lipstick and her cowboy hat, then pulled on her cowboy boots and left the cabin for the barn. There was no sign of Dr.

Clayton's truck. Maybe he'd already come and gone. She walked inside, hoping that wasn't true.

"Good morning," she said when she saw Wes coming out of the stall next to Chief's. Last night she'd noticed that Fran's husband was most likely twenty-four or twenty-five, just slightly older than his wife. But unlike Fran, he didn't have her friendly disposition. Talk about opposites.

"Morning," he muttered. "Sorry I wasn't here when you arrived yesterday. I was in town checking on supplies to be delivered."

"No problem."

"I didn't realize anyone else had been hired to go on the trail rides with the horses. Usually the family handles that."

She supposed the talk his grandfather had given him last night had wrought a few changes. But though he'd said the right words to her just now, her intuition told her he still wasn't happy with the situation.

"I think it was a last-minute decision between my grandfather and John for me to be given a job on the dude ranch." Except that it wasn't true. She'd been hired when she'd come to the dude ranch in the Spring, but it appeared John hadn't said anything at that time. "It's a great privilege for me."

His head jerked up. "You know my grandfather?"

Why did that bother him so much? "He and mine were best friends growing up. John is doing me a favor letting me work here this summer and I'm very grateful."

The other man couldn't hide his irritation and didn't

try. She didn't understand it, but knew to give him a wide berth. Tracey couldn't help but wonder how Fran handled him at times like this. The answer, of course, was that his wife was in love with him, and Wes was attractive, like the other Hunter men.

"Everyone around here is at breakfast," he reminded her. "If you haven't eaten yet, now's the time."

Good grief. He *wanted* her to leave. "I realize that, but I thought I'd check on Chief first."

"I've already done that, so it won't be necessary. He's fine."

Tracey had to count to ten. "I understand it'll be two weeks before we'll find out if he's fully recovered. Do you know if Dr. Clayton has been here yet?"

"Nope." Wrong question. "It seems *you're* the one who told Granddad there was a new vet in Ravalli County."

Strike one against her. She wasn't wrong about his antagonism toward her. The question was why he felt so threatened. Tracey had picked up a lot from teaching children. Wes had become very defensive and was blaming her. Though she probably couldn't alleviate the problem, she decided to give it one more try.

"When your grandfather couldn't reach Dr. Cruz, we were both desperate, because Chief was in pain. That's when I mentioned passing the Clayton Veterinary Hospital after I left Stevensville."

Wes's brown eyes took on what she thought was a strange glitter, but maybe it was a trick of the light. "You're new here and would be wise to realize Chief is my horse. I'm the one who determines his care and knows what's best for him."

Did Wes mean he actually *owned* the horse? John had told her she could pick out any one she wanted. "Grady mentioned as much." Somewhere there'd been a disconnect.

"One more thing for you to know. Dr. Cruz is our dude ranch vet, Tracey. When he's back in his office on Monday, he'll be the one to finish Chief's treatment."

Whoa. If there was some problem between Wes and his grandfather over the choice of vet, she didn't dare get into it, and changed the subject.

"Yesterday I got acquainted with most of the horses, but Grady told me there are several I still haven't seen. Would you mind showing them to me so I can pick out one to ride?"

"Not at all. But I think I know the one for you. Fancy Pants is the bay and a great mare. I'll be exercising them in the corral a little later where you can get a good look at her."

Tracey had already done that. It appeared Wes was doing everything to put her in her place. She certainly hadn't expected to meet this degree of animosity over the vet incident and knew she needed to tread carefully. "Then I'll come back. Thank you."

"Sure."

Since he'd made it clear he didn't want her looking at Chief or the other horses right now, she started walking back to her cabin and pulled the granola bar out of her pocket. While she munched on it, she saw a red truck in the distance coming toward the barn. Her steps slowed and her heart did a huge kick.

When Dr. Clayton reached her, he lowered his window. "Good morning."

It was, now. "Good morning."

"How's our patient?"

"I haven't seen him yet. Wes told me he was fine and suggested I go to breakfast before it was too late to be served."

"That's interesting."

They could read each other's minds. "I thought so, too."

"Is that where you're headed now?"

"No. I had a snack a few minutes ago."

"If you have time, would you like to take a look at him with me? I could use your calming influence while I inspect his hoof."

"I have plenty of time."

"Do you mind if I call you Tracey?"

"As if I would."

She knew her feelings for him were growing too fast. In the short time since meeting him—heavens, was it only last night?—Tracey had the impression she was suddenly experiencing life in glorious Technicolor. He seemed bigger than life to her, stronger, more wonderful.

Oh, yes. He *was* definitely wonderful.

Chapter Three

Doctor Clayton's eyes roamed over her features. "What a beautiful day."

"Isn't it?" Sunshine filled a blue sky. Her heart wouldn't stop thudding.

Thrilled that he wanted her with him, she waited while he parked the truck and got out with his bag. In a black Stetson, jeans and a blue denim shirt he was so striking, she was in danger of staring. Together they walked into the barn toward the third stall.

Wes came out of another stall a little farther down. "Dr. Clayton..." By the tautness of his features, Tracey could tell he hadn't expected to see the vet show up this soon.

"Good morning, Mr. Hunter. As you know, I'm here on your grandfather's orders to soak Chief's hoof and put on a new poultice. Tracey's going to help me." He turned to her. "I'll fill this bucket with some warm water and get started."

"I'll do it for you."

"Thanks." He handed it to her. She could tell Wes

didn't want her doing anything, but he couldn't very well interfere.

When she came back, she set it next to the vet, who'd unwrapped the soiled poultice. She squatted next to him. "It drained a lot during the night."

"That's exactly the result we wanted." His smile sent a wave of warmth through her body. "The infection has built up, but we're getting rid of it now." He reached for more Epsom salts to put in the water, then lowered the hoof into the bucket. "That feels good, doesn't it, buddy?" he said to the horse.

His gentleness and professionalism mesmerized Tracey. "Look at that," she said softly. "His ears are up. You've made a friend."

"My former boss, Hannah, used to say it was one of the perks of being a vet. I discovered she was right."

"Chief is the horse I would have liked to ride while I'm here this summer, but I understand he belongs to Wes. In any case I hope he has a full recovery."

"For both your sakes, I want the same thing. We'll know soon enough." The vet shot her a sideways glance. "Tell me about yourself. How did you happen to start working here?" he asked in a quiet voice.

"My grandfather and Mr. Hunter grew up in Polson and are still best friends."

"The Flathead area is one of my favorite places."

"I was born there and I love it. But after teaching sixth grade all year, I wanted to get away for the summer. Riding is my passion. Grandpa suggested I try to get hired here to help on the trail rides."

"I met with Mr. Hunter this morning. He's very grateful he took you on."

"That's good to hear."

"I learned that Chief happens to be his favorite and most expensive horse. He didn't mention that Wes owned him."

"One of the other staff told me that before Wes told me himself this morning."

"Maybe it's just the horse he prefers while he's working at the stable."

"Maybe." But both of them knew there was a lot more to the story.

"John told me you're a valuable employee for noticing the limp."

"I don't know about that." She studied his arresting profile. "Why did you leave your practice in Missoula?"

"The owner died a little over two months ago."

"Oh, dear."

"Though I could have bought her practice, I preferred to set up my own on our family's ranch. Unfortunately, I've lost a fair number of patients by moving."

"But I don't blame you for wanting to be with your family. John told me yours is a big cattle ranch. You'd have enough patients without ever having to leave the property."

He chuckled. "You're right about that. We'll see. These things take time. It might interest you to know Mr. Hunter is my first new client since my move. That's thanks to you."

She bet John didn't know that, and if Wes had his way, today's visit would be the end of it. "What a coincidence that I happened to notice your hospital yesterday. I'm happy John called you."

"Frankly, so am I."

Tracey couldn't learn enough about him. "Do you come from a big family?"

"Three brothers. Two of them are married. What about you?"

"I have one married brother who's a forest ranger. My grandfather lives with my parents now."

"You're very fortunate they're alive. My own dad passed away, but I'm lucky to still have my mother."

"I'm sorry for your loss," Tracey whispered. "How long ago was it?"

"Several years. He had the most influence on me to become a vet." With that revelation, Roce lifted Chief's hoof from the bucket and prepared a new poultice. After wrapping it, he glanced at her. "Thanks for helping me."

"I wanted to make sure he was healing. Until we know how he fares, I'll have to pick another horse. My job starts in the morning when the first tourists arrive."

The vet put things back in his bag and got to his feet. "What will you do with the rest of your day?"

"Not a lot. I'm new to this area and plan to look around. I'll probably drive into Hamilton to do a few errands."

"If you're free, would you like to go to lunch? I don't need to get back to the hospital until this afternoon."

Tracey was so excited she didn't know how to contain it. "Let me empty this bucket and I'll meet you out in front."

She had to pass Wes to reach the drain. He ignored her. Under normal circumstances he ought to have been the one to take care of it, but he'd elected not to go near the vet. After she'd rinsed out the bucket and put it back in Chief's stall, she walked outside.

To her surprise, Grady came hurrying up to her. "There you are! I was hoping to catch up with you. Do you want to go for a horseback ride? It would be the perfect time to try out the horse you'll be riding all summer."

He meant the mare Wes had already picked out for her. "Thanks, but I have other plans for today. Grady Cox? I guess you haven't met Dr. Clayton, who's been treating Chief's hoof. He runs a veterinary hospital near Stevensville." She turned to the doctor. "Grady's a college student in Missoula who has worked here several summers, managing the horses."

"Lucky you, Grady. It's nice to meet you."

"You, too."

The younger man switched his gaze to Tracey. "Maybe we can go riding another time then."

"Of course."

Once he'd headed for the barn, Tracey followed the vet around to the passenger side of his truck. He opened the door so she could climb in the cab. When their eyes met, she knew something earthshaking was happening to her.

After getting in his side and starting the engine, he turned to her. "What are you in the mood for?"

"I missed breakfast, so I'm starting to get an appetite. A granola bar doesn't last all that long."

She heard a chuckle. "Since I wanted to talk to Mr. Hunter early, I left the house without eating, so I'm hungry, too. Let's drive into town and see what we can find."

He drove by farms and orchards until they entered the town of five thousand. After passing different stores and businesses, they both suddenly cried out as they spotted a sign that said Breakfast All Day. After they'd broken into laughter, he pulled up in front of the family-style restaurant. "That was easy."

They both went to the restroom to wash their hands before finding a table. The waitress poured them coffee and took their order. Tracey hadn't been this happy for over two and a half years. Though Jeff had been killed eighteen months ago, she'd worried about him for the entire year he'd first been deployed.

Today she felt a new lightness in her heart. It had everything to do with the gorgeous man seated across from her. His hazel eyes shone like gemstones. He'd removed his hat, revealing his dark blond hair. A large-animal vet like him spent a lot of time in the sun, as evidenced by his bronzed complexion. His male beauty was something to behold.

The waitress obviously thought so, too. Tracey might as well have not existed while the other woman chatted about how she'd never seen him in here before. After dropping her name, she said she hoped he'd come again.

"Maybe since you'll be treating Chief for another

ten days, 'Cassie' will get her wish," Tracey teased after the woman walked away.

A half smile broke out on his face. "It could happen, as long as you're with me."

Her breath caught at his comment, but there was something he needed to know. At first she hadn't intended to tell him, because she didn't want to interfere with John and his grandson, but this was too important.

"Dr. Clayton—" she began.

"Call me Roce. It's pronounced like Rossi, but spelled with an *e*.

"That's good to know. I've never heard that name before."

"It's short for Rocelin, an old English name."

His name was as unique as the man himself. "What I wanted to say was that this morning Wes confronted me in the barn."

His expression sobered. "In what regard?"

"I wanted to check on Chief, but he said he'd already done it. He also told me that Dr. Cruz was the vet and would be taking care of Chief from now on."

Roce nodded. "I appreciate you telling me, but I was already aware there was a problem. Suffice it to say Mr. Hunter made it clear he employed me. I'm afraid Wes will have to deal with his grandfather if he's unhappy."

"I'm relieved then, because we both know he's unhappy and isn't worried about showing it."

"How true. That's one troubled young man."

"I couldn't agree more." They left the conversation there.

After enjoying another cup of coffee, Cassie brought

them, Roce put some bills on the table. "You said you had errands to run. Ready to do them?"

"All I really wanted to do was buy some treats for the horses. Today I've got to choose the one I want to ride this summer. Wes informed me this morning he's already chosen one for me. She's a bay mare, his pick."

"He likes being in charge."

"True. If she's the one I ride to keep the peace, a treat might help us become friends sooner."

"Then let's do it."

They left the restaurant and walked to the truck. He drove to the feed store they'd passed earlier and he took her inside. They wandered around until they found what she was looking for.

"My horse, Spirit, loves Paddock Cakes," Tracey commented.

Roce darted an amused glance her way. "Of course he does. Let's add some lactose-free Probio snacks to aid the digestion of those gummy frogs." She laughed as he reached for them, and they walked to the counter to pay for everything.

Soon they headed back to the ranch. She put the sack of treats in her purse.

"Where do you want me to drop you?"

"If you would let me off by the corral, that would be perfect. Wes said he'd be exercising the horses I haven't seen yet. I'll have to find one to ride before morning. He'll expect me to pick the bay, of course."

"Want some help?"

She took a quick breath. "I'd be thrilled, but I don't dare impose on your time."

"I'm not in a hurry."

He pulled to a stop and they got out. Tracey counted seven horses in the corral. She saw Wes standing against the corral fencing. In a whisper she said, "Yup. There's the mare."

"Let's take a look at her first."

There was no question Wes was glaring at them when they entered the corral. Without being asked, he deliberately reached for the bay and led her over to Tracey, ignoring Roce. "This is Fancy Pants."

She'd already examined her yesterday, but made a pretense of doing it again. While Roce did his own inspection afterward, she turned to Wes, who'd been watching them like a cat ready to pounce on a mouse.

"Before dinner I'll take Fancy Pants for a ride." If Tracey had said anything else, there would have been an ugly scene. She could almost taste the venom coming from Wes. She didn't want that. "See you later."

Once again Roce nodded to the other man before the two of them headed for his truck. After he climbed in behind the wheel, he looked down at her from the open window as he'd done earlier. "The mare appears in good health. You'll know a lot more about her when you take her for a ride."

"You're right. Thank you for breakfast."

"My pleasure. I'll be back here at six thirty in the morning."

Tracey would be living for it.

"If I'm held up for some reason, let's exchange cell phone numbers so we can stay in touch."

She nodded, thrilled he'd suggested it. They traded phones to put in their numbers.

"See you soon, Tracey."

As he drove off, she walked to her cabin, hoping Grady wouldn't see her and try to monopolize her time. Before long she would have to have a heart-to-heart talk with her grandfather over the situation brewing between Wes and John. If he had any advice, she wanted to hear it, but that conversation could wait another day.

For a little while all she wanted to do was savor the time she'd just spent with Roce Clayton.

ROCE KNEW TROUBLE from the first moment Wes Hunter had exploded on the scene in the barn last evening. He feared Tracey was caught in the middle of an unpleasant situation. After watching Wes in action just now, he made up his mind to keep a close eye on what was going on behind the scenes.

Once he'd reached the house, he let Daisy outside, then brought her back in. After pouring more water in her dish, he worked in his office. He had some phone calls to return from patients in the Missoula area. There was also a mountain of mail to go through that he'd retrieved from his box at the post office in Stevensville.

An hour later he came across a letter from the Bitterroot-Sapphire Animal Festival being held in a few days in Hamilton.

Dear Dr. Clayton,

Our committee is hoping to assemble as many local veterinarians as possible who would be

willing to help or be on call during our three-day
festival over the June 8-10 weekend. If you could
give us the times you might be available, there
will be a small remuneration for your service.

That was four days away. Roce's mind was already
racing ahead.

Festival organizers have put out the following
health advisory to those who bring animals, asking that they be conscious of the risks and take
simple precautions.

Roce read the advisory. But the fact that decided
him to help out lay at the feet of a certain enticing female working on the Rocky Point Dude Ranch. After
being with her today, he knew in his gut she was attracted to him, too, and he thought he would invite her
to attend some of the festival events with him.

Excited to have another reason to see her away from
the dude ranch, he emailed his response, then took
Daisy with him to his mom's for Sunday dinner.

Everyone had congregated except their youngest
brother, Toly, who was still single and on the rodeo circuit. When Roce walked into the living room, Libby
shouted for joy and ran over to play with Daisy.

Eli sat on the couch with Brianna and Jasmine, the
wife of their oldest brother, Wymon. Everyone fought
to hold Eli and Brianna's new baby. Just two weeks
old, little Stephen, named after their father, Stephen
Clayton, was adorable, and the family was overjoyed.

"How's the new Clayton Ranch vet?" Wymon asked, giving Roce a hug.

"That depends. Since Mom hasn't announced dinner yet, let's go in the den for a minute. I want to talk to you about something."

"Sounds serious."

"It could be."

They went into their father's study and he shut the doors. "You know the ranchers around here better than anyone. What can you tell me about John Hunter? He made it big in oil and owns the Rocky Point Dude Ranch outside Hamilton. He said he met you at a rodeo last year."

"That's right." Wymon sat on a corner of the old oak desk. "He's well-known and revered. I'm biased, from a personal standpoint, because he was an early contributor to our coalition's agenda to reintroduce grizzly bears to the Sapphire Mountains."

"I'm glad to hear it. Do you know anything about his family?"

"I've met Sheldon, who helps his father buy the horses they use on the ranch. We've talked several times. He seems like a good man, too." Wymon cocked his head. "What's this all about?"

Roce wasted no time telling him what had happened last evening. "Wes is Sheldon's son and married to a girl named Fran. Wes told me under no uncertain terms that Dr. Cruz, who's from Darby, will be taking over Chief's care starting tomorrow. That goes exactly against what John told me."

Wymon shook his head. "Obviously, the grandson

is making trouble for you already. I wonder why. How old is he?"

"Mid-twenties maybe. In my opinion he was irrationally upset that Tracey was the one who noticed Chief's limp in the first place. He claims it's his horse, and he was in town when she went to the corral to check out the horse she wanted to ride."

"Tracey?"

"Yes. Tracey Marcroft. She's an elementary schoolteacher from Polson. She was hired to help with the trail rides this summer. I learned that she grew up around horses and even did a little barrel racing. She picked out Chief as the best of the lot. Her grandfather is close friends with John. That's how she got the job.

"But instead of Wes being glad she saw what was wrong with the horse, he was so cold. Dr. Cruz wasn't available, so John Hunter called me. Now I have to ask why Wes is that intent on Dr. Cruz taking over, when it's John's decision. Something doesn't feel right."

"I agree." Wymon got to his feet. "Though I don't know anything about the grandson, I have a source in the police department. He'll tell me if the guy has had any trouble with the law. Let me see if I can reach him right now."

He pulled out his phone and made the call. Roce listened and was surprised to hear his brother ask his friend to do a search on Dr. Cruz, too. After a few minutes, Wymon hung up and looked at Roce.

"He'll get back to me if he finds any information."

"It's probably a long shot. In any event, I owe you, bro," Roce said.

"Happy to be of help. Let me know how things turn out when you drive there in the morning. If anything goes wrong, I've got your back."

"Thanks."

They rejoined the others for dinner. Toly phoned from Oklahoma to say hello to everyone. Their brother was a former tie-down roper turned expert team roper on his way to winning the pro rodeo finals in Las Vegas in December. After they'd all had their chance to talk to him, Roce went home with Daisy.

Everyone begged him to stay, but he had Tracey Marcroft on his mind and couldn't concentrate. Depending on her work schedule, he might be seeing her early in the morning. If he didn't, he'd leave a message for her at the dude ranch front desk and ask her to call him when she could.

Before he went to bed, he had a call from Luis, the Clayton ranch foreman. "What's up, Luis?"

"The boys brought a cow down from the pasture who needs to give birth, but can't. She's in the barn."

"I'll be right there."

He hung up and patted Daisy's head. "Got to go. Take care of the place for me. I'll be back as soon as I can."

The second he walked into the stall with his bag, he realized the calf's buttocks were coming out first instead of its front legs and head. This was a breech birth.

He petted the mom. "I'll help you." But it would be a struggle because she couldn't push it out by herself.

After doing all the preparations, he had to reach into the uterus to reposition the calf and push as far as he could. Eventually, he located a hind leg. He flexed the hock enough to bring the leg up to the roof of the uterus.

"Ah—there's the foot." He brought it up over the pelvic rim, then repeated the process with the other leg. Reaching for his calving chains, he put a half-inch knot above the fetlock and below the hocks.

"Here we go." He pulled hard with the cow's contractions. Suddenly the calf was free and he cleared the airway to get her breathing.

"Look at that," Luis said with a smile. "She's fit as a fiddle. If your dad could see you now, he'd be bursting with pride."

"Thanks, Luis."

Roce returned to his house near midnight. To his relief, he'd been able to save the calf. Breech births were tricky, but now mom and baby were doing fine. It was always a good feeling.

He showered and went to bed, excited for morning to come. Until he fell asleep, all he could think about was Tracey. She had the most perfect mouth. He longed to taste it. The rest of her was pretty perfect, too, from her softly rounded chin to her shapely legs.

He couldn't understand for the life of him why Wes Hunter would have been so upset that Tracey had taken Chief for a walk without his permission. Roce thought there had to be more to his animosity than just that. Clearly, Wes didn't want another vet looking after Chief. Maybe that was the key, and he blamed Tracey for suggesting Roce's name to his grandfather.

Then again, it was also possible that he resented

someone outside the Hunter family being hired to do the trail rides. If they were an exclusive club, then Wes could be angry with his grandfather for hiring her.

Whatever the answer, Roce intended to get to the bottom of it. For him the situation had become personal.

Because she has become important to you, Clayton.

Chapter Four

Tracey's work schedule consisted of eating breakfast with the rest of the staff cafeteria-style anywhere between 6:00 and 7:30 a.m. After that, she was to report to the stables at eight, ready to help with guests and take on assignments as laid out by Wes.

After her shower, she put on a dark green pullover and jeans, and arrived in the dining room. Roce would be coming to check on Chief at six thirty and she didn't want to miss him.

Grady walked in at twenty after six. Though four other girls who worked for the ranch were seated at various tables, he made a beeline for Tracey with his tray. "I was hoping to see you in here."

"How are you, Grady?"

"Terrific. It's your first day on the job. Are you excited?"

"Yes. How about you?"

"It's a means to an end."

"What do you plan to do when you've graduated?"

"Hopefully, go for an MBA."

"Good for you." She finished her bacon and drank the rest of her coffee before getting to her feet.

"Hey—where are you going?"

"I don't mean to be rude, but I need to get to the barn early to see about the horse I'll be riding."

"Wes told me he chose Fancy Pants for you." That didn't surprise Tracey. "She's a nice, docile mare."

"She seems to be, but I haven't ridden her yet." She'd decided not to ride her until today because she didn't like being manipulated.

"What's your hurry? We don't have to be there until eight."

"True, but I want to take my time getting her used to my saddle and bridle." She put on her cowboy hat. "I'll see you later."

Tracey walked back to her cabin to freshen up before heading for the barn. As she was on her way out the door she heard her phone ring. Her heart raced when she saw the caller ID.

"Roce?"

"Hi!"

"Are you already at the ranch?"

"I'm just driving in and wanted to pass on some information to you before we see each other. Wymon's friend at police headquarters contacted him early this morning. Nothing showed up on a Dr. Cruz from Darby.

"But Wesley Hunter, twenty-five years old, from Hamilton, Montana, and Ramon Cruz, twenty-five, also from Hamilton, had some minor infractions for drunkenness two years earlier. And here's the worst part—three months ago Wes was arrested on a stolen horse charge but didn't serve jail time."

"You're kidding."

"John Hunter has to be covering up something to allow his grandson to still be working on the dude ranch. I don't like it, Tracey."

"Neither do I. You knew something was wrong. You have amazing instincts."

"Wymon's friend said you'd have to get a court order from a judge to see the details of that arrest and the outcome. This guy not only has a serious police record, but a hot temper to prove it, as you've found out."

Tracey gripped the phone tighter. "He was rude to all of us, but especially toward his grandfather. Frankly, I was appalled at the way he treated him two nights ago."

"It was ugly, but now we know Wes Hunter has real problems and we need to be careful around him. I'll be there in five minutes."

Her heart did a double flip when she walked outside and saw his red truck pull up near the barn. Perfect timing. A dozen horses, including Fancy Pants and two ponies, had already been taken out to the corral. All were bridled and saddled except for the mare. That meant Wes was up and on the job.

Roce jumped down and waited for her to join him. When his eyes played over her, she could hardly breathe. "Green is a great color on you, but then you look good in anything."

"Flattery this early in the morning?" she teased with a pounding heart.

"When it's deserved." He picked up his bag. "Are you ready?"

She knew exactly what he was asking. Anything might happen when they went inside. Some sort of confrontation with Wes was inevitable. "I'm anxious to see how Chief is doing."

Together they entered the barn. There was no sign of Wes as they walked to the third stall. She blinked.

It was empty!

Angry heat suffused her face. Where had Wes taken Chief? Where was the stable manager hiding? She bet Grady was in his confidence, since he'd known she'd be riding Fancy Pants. He hadn't said a word at breakfast except to try and assure her that the mare was a gentle horse. If she didn't miss her guess, he'd wanted to detain her, possibly to give Wes time to take the horse away.

Tracey felt her blood pressure rise. If John had told Wes that she had done some barrel racing in the past, then he'd chosen the mare as an insult. So many negative thoughts converged in her mind at once, she was at a loss.

When she lifted her eyes to Roce, he shook his head as if to tell her not to react. In the next breath, he pulled out his cell phone. She knew he was calling John. After a brief conversation, he hung up.

"Mr. Hunter wants me to come to his office."

"Then you have to go." She was afraid this meant no more visits with Roce to brighten her mornings. Already she felt deprived.

He studied her for a moment. "What time are you off work each day?"

"Five o'clock on weekdays, two o'clock Saturdays. Sunday is my day off."

"I'll give you a call this evening."

"Please do, Roce. I'm dying to know what's going on."

"You're not alone," he muttered, the first sign he'd shown that he didn't like this situation any more than she did. "Enjoy your first day."

That would be impossible now. "Good luck, Roce," she said.

He walked one way while she headed for the tack room to get her gear. Once she'd lugged everything out to the corral, she saddled and bridled the mare. After a few turns around the corral it was clear this horse was meant for someone who hadn't been on one before or who was nervous around horses.

Tracey rode her outside the corral so the horse would get used to her weight and signals. As far as she knew, there wouldn't be any long trail rides today. But the tourists could ride around the five-hundred-acre ranch and enjoy the gorgeous mountains.

Before long she went back to the corral. By now, John's other grandson, Rod, and his wife, Colette, had emerged from the barn on their horses. The three of them talked while they anticipated the tourists who would show up at eight. If the couple knew what was going on, they didn't show it. Wes followed on foot and leaned against the corral fencing.

He shot Tracey a glance. "How does the mare feel?"

Was he trying to intimidate her, or was it an attempt to be friendly? She couldn't tell.

"Nice and docile," she said, repeating Grady's words.

"Good. We're not completely full today so you'll only have to deal with one family. I've made the assignments. The Briscoes from North Carolina have two kids who've never ridden before. You'd be the right choice to take them around."

"I'd be happy to." She refused to give him the satisfaction of knowing how much she disliked him. "How old are they?"

"Nine and ten. They should do well on Patty Cake and Raspberry, the roan and the chestnut out there."

"Those ponies are so cute."

She didn't hear his response because several families suddenly came hurrying toward the corral. The children ran ahead and climbed on the fence to get a better look at the horses. This was Tracey's cue.

She walked over to them. "Hi! I'm Tracey. You must be the Briscoes. What are your names?"

"Sarah," said the little girl.

"Pete," the boy replied.

"I hear you've never ridden a horse before." They shook their heads. She eyed their parents, who were coming up behind them. "Why don't you all come with me and I'll help you find the right horses."

"Can we ride the ponies?"

"They're out here just for you. That chestnut-colored one is Patty Cake. The red roan is Raspberry. When we reach them, give them one of these." She reached in her pocket for the horse treats and unwrapped them. "If you put one on your palm, the pony will take it and eat it. Then you'll be friends for life."

Their father's wide grin gave her a lift. She knew she was going to enjoy the time spent with this family from the East. After a fun ride with the children, she'd get to talk to Roce. How amazing that last Saturday morning, she didn't even know the doctor cowboy from the Clayton ranch existed.

AFTER ROCE TOOK a seat in John's office, the older man leaned forward. "I'm aware of what has happened. At five thirty this morning, Wes loaded Chief in one of our trailers and drove him off the ranch. Sheldon happened to be up early and followed him to Dr. Cruz's surgery in Darby.

"It grieves both of us that Wes overrode my decision for you to treat Chief. My grandson's inexcusable behavior has resulted in an unpleasant situation for all of us. Sheldon and I will be dealing with Wes before the day is out."

"I'm fine with that, but I'm curious—why didn't he want me to at least finish the treatment?"

"It's a long story. One of Wes's closest friends is Dr. Cruz's son."

Roce nodded. "So, it's an allegiance thing."

"Partly. I also think Wes feels he lost face by not noticing Chief's limp, and is determined to show me he'll make it right. But be assured, I'll pay you the full amount regardless of how long you were here."

Roce felt the man's sincerity, but felt sorry for him,

too. "I'm not worried about that. These things happen in families and are usually straightened out given time. Tracey didn't realize Chief was Wes's horse."

John's head lifted abruptly. "Wes told her that?"

"Yes."

"Nothing could be further from the truth. I'm saddened that Tracey has to be involved in this. Under the circumstances, I'm going to have to tell you something in strictest confidence, because you deserve to know everything.

"Wes grew up expecting his father and me to give him whatever he wanted. He thought he deserved a car at sixteen, which didn't happen. Later he believed he was ready for an important position at Hunter Oil. Yet he had to drop out of college because he couldn't keep up his grades. During that period he also developed a drinking problem.

"Sheldon talked him into working here on the dude ranch, suggesting that he'd be able to run it one day. We thought that was the incentive he needed. For a time, it seemed to work. He quit drinking and married Fran. I'd hoped he was on track for a good life at last. But three months ago he was caught stealing a valuable broodmare off a ranch in Conner, about a half hour from here."

That *was* serious. "For what reason?"

"Who knows what goes on in his mind? To sell, maybe? But due to the Ravalli county sheriff's quick intervention, he was caught and the mare returned. I called my attorney to represent him in court.

"There's something terribly wrong with my grandson to think he could steal a valuable horse and get away with it. No doubt he had help, but the detective assigned to his case hasn't been able to implicate anyone else."

"So Dr. Cruz's son is in the clear?"

"Ramon had an alibi for the night of the theft."

"You're in a very painful situation. I'm sorry, John."

The older man nodded. "As I'm sure you know, being a veterinarian, Montana's Senate Bill 214 requires that a person convicted of livestock theft pay a minimum fine of five thousand dollars. The bill also says that if a jail sentence is deferred, offenders must contribute a mandatory 416 hours of community service. In addition, any equipment used in the crime, like a truck and horse trailer, is confiscated.

"Because this was Wes's first offense, my attorney prevailed on the judge to let him do his community service with me for the whole summer, 416 hours with no salary. His sentence also included going to therapy once a week.

"In the fall, when he can start working for wages again, he'll have to pay his father back for the five-thousand-dollar loan, plus buy him a truck and trailer. The equipment he stole was Sheldon's, and it was confiscated."

Though this detailed explanation answered Roce's questions, he was more concerned than ever for Tracey now, as she had to deal with Wes on a daily basis. He was obviously dealing with some deep-seated issues. "What a shame, John. You have my word this information will stay between the two of us. Thank you for calling me. It meant a lot. If you ever need me on an emergency basis, I'll be happy to come. See you again soon."

After leaving the ranch, he stopped at a store in Hamilton to do some grocery shopping and fill the gas tank. Once back home, he phoned Wymon and told him everything. He trusted his older brother with his life.

"Wes Hunter is a bad customer," Wymon declared.

"I'm afraid John thinks he is, too, but is still trying to help him all he can. I just wanted to thank you for making that call to your friend. I'm concerned that Tracey has to work with him every day."

"That's the second time you've mentioned her name. What aren't you telling me?"

Roce's pulse picked up speed. "Have you got a whole day?"

There was a pregnant pause. "I never thought I'd hear that come out of you."

He closed his eyes for minute. "Neither did I."

"Well, what do you know.

"That's what I said the first time I saw you and Jasmine together. I hardly recognized you. My big brother in love was quite a sight."

"It appears your move to the ranch was inspirational in more ways than one."

"I'm still reeling. Just promise me—"

"Don't worry." Wymon broke in on him. "It's your secret to tell when you're ready."

"These are early days."

"That's what I kept telling myself after finding every reason under the sun to be with Jasmine."

"I hear you. Thanks. Talk to you later."

He hung up and headed for the barn to see how the mother and new calf were doing. Satisfied all was well, he drove back to his house to take care of Daisy and fix lunch.

That afternoon, two new patients came by the hospital without appointments. Being this close to the highway was paying off in promising ways. When Hannah had passed away, he hadn't been able to imagine a day like this. Roce owed a debt to his parents for helping him realize his dream.

He tended to a boxer with redness in the ear canal. The other dog, a sheltie, had diarrhea and needed to be dewormed.

By five thirty he'd showered and shaved, and he phoned Tracey, eager to hear her voice. She answered on the third ring. "Roce?"

He wasn't mistaken about the excitement in her tone. "Where are you?"

"In my cabin, getting cleaned up."

He gripped his phone tighter. "Do I want to know how things went today? You know what I mean."

"Wes was what you would call 'civil' today. I was thankful for that. And I had a good time with the children. They loved the ponies. It's fun to watch them feed them treats."

"I can imagine. Do you have any extra duties this evening?"

"No. I'm through."

That sounded definite. "How would you like me to pick you up? We'll make dinner at my house and talk."

"I'd love it."

Her answer was more than he could have hoped for. "I'll be there in twenty minutes."

"I'm in cabin two. It'll be good to talk to you about everything."

"I feel the same way."

AFTER SHE HUNG UP, Tracey hurried into the shower. Afterward, she changed her mind three times about what to wear while she blow-dried her hair.

In the end, she chose a new pair of pleated khaki pants and a periwinkle-colored sweater with long sleeves and a round neck. She slid her feet into leather sandals and applied a pink frost lipstick. It had been so long since she'd wanted to dress up for a man.

If Roce had any doubts about Tracey's feelings for him, their last, short phone conversation would have erased them. While she put on her gold stud earrings with the violet stones, she heard the knock on the door. She grabbed her purse and hurried to open it. Her spirits plummeted when she found Grady standing there.

"Hi, Tracey. Wow. You look fantastic!"

"Thank you."

"I was hoping to catch you and see if you wanted to go to a movie with me in Hamilton."

She clung to the door handle and took a deep breath. Admittedly, he didn't have her phone number to prepare her, but she wished he'd gotten the hint that she wasn't interested.

"That's very nice of you, but I'm afraid I have other plans for this evening." Over his shoulder, she could see

Roce's red truck approaching. "Here's my date now." She pulled the door shut.

Grady looked behind him and frowned. "I didn't realize you and Dr. Clayton were going out. Wes was right. That new vet doesn't waste time, does he?"

The person who didn't waste time was Grady, who had two big marks against him at this point. Besides being intimidated by Wes, who ran the show, he was like a young bull, hitting the gate with his horns, hell-bent on getting out of the chute no matter the obstacle.

Roce climbed down from the cab, dressed in a silky, dark brown shirt and beige pants. Every time Tracey saw him, she got a fluttery sensation in her chest.

"How are you this evening, Grady?" he asked in a mild-mannered tone.

She would never forget the shocked look on the younger man's face. "Dr. Clayton..." His glance slid away. "See you later, Tracey."

The second he left, she started toward Roce, who didn't say anything. Instead he walked around to the passenger door and opened it for her. She accidentally brushed against him to get in and was assailed by the scent of the soap he'd used in the shower.

Within seconds he'd started the engine and they drove down the track. "Thank heaven you came when you did, Roce," she blurted.

"You know the problem, don't you?" He flicked her an all-encompassing glance. "A woman whose violet eyes are more stunning than her earrings is hard on the male of the species."

She burst into laughter in order to cover her secret delight at his words. "How was your day?"

"I acquired two more patients who noticed my sign."

"That's wonderful! Interestingly enough, my eye was caught by your house before I read the sign."

"Why is that?"

"My mom used to read stories to me before I could read myself. Some of my favorites were written by Laura Ingalls Wilder. Your house reminds me of the cover on her first book, *Little House in the Big Woods*. It's the reason I slowed down. Only then did I realize it was a veterinary hospital."

"Long ago it served as a sheep station. My brothers helped me restore it and add on a second level."

"Being good at building stuff seems to go with the territory when you're raised on a ranch. The people in my family can build or fix just about anything. My mom's a great plumber."

She heard Roce's chuckle before he slowed down and turned off the highway into the small parking lot. Tracey got out of the truck, eager to see where he worked.

Before he unlocked the front door, she could hear barking, and turned to him. "One of your patients?"

"No. It's my dog, Daisy." The second he opened it, the border collie–Lab mix ran to him, then sniffed at Tracey.

"Oh, Roce—what happened to her front leg?"

"Hannah found her in a trap and had to amputate. But she survived and is as active as any dog. She used to be Hannah's, but when Hannah died, her family didn't want a dog, so I adopted her and brought her to live with me."

"She's adorable. All black with a white front like a tuxedo. Her three paws are white, too. You precious thing." Tracey hunkered down to scratch her head and pet her. The dog started licking her hands.

"Better watch out. Daisy loves the attention and won't leave you alone."

"I should be so lucky. Did Hannah give her that name?"

He nodded. "She was on a hike with her husband. They'd just walked through a meadow of wild daisies when they found the dog in a nearby ravine, with no collar. She was half-dead from the loss of blood. They immediately transported her to the hospital in Missoula. Hannah put out notices, but no one came to claim Daisy. Finders, keepers…"

Tracey rubbed behind her ears. "Who would put out a trap to hurt a dear dog like you?"

"Someone hoping to bag a bear."

"How horrible."

Roce stood with his hands on his hips, grinning down at her. "When you're ready, I'll give you the full tour. It'll take a total of two minutes."

She straightened. "Come on, Daisy. Show me where you eat." The dog managed beautifully, hopping on three legs. "Does she even know she's missing a limb?"

"She had problems at first. It's called proprioception. She had to figure out where her body was in space and how to balance—kind of like the bubble in a level."

"Well, she's certainly conquered that problem."

He led them through the front room, with its couch and fireplace. It had been turned into a reception area containing a coffee table and several chairs. A TV in the corner made it a perfect room for pet owners waiting to see the doctor.

Next he took her down the hall to a cheery, modernized kitchen. Daisy hurried over to her water bowl.

"My biggest challenge is to protect her limbs."

"In what way?"

"Make certain she doesn't overdo it. Otherwise there could be too much pressure on her joints that could bring on arthritis."

"We don't want that, do we, Daisy?" The dog came right back to her for another pat.

Roce smiled. "The bathroom and surgery are down the hall if you want to explore. I'll start making the burritos. I hope you like pulled pork."

"Mmm. Sounds like you're a great cook."

"Hardly. But I've been a bachelor so long, I've had to learn how to make a meal or starve to death."

She left him long enough to explore the rest of the main floor. Daisy followed her. They passed a staircase and a bathroom next to a small bedroom. On the opposite side of the hallway, she found the surgery. Tracey turned on the switch to discover a state-of-the-art examination room. Through another door, she glimpsed his office.

Delicious smells filtered through the hall as she made her way back to the kitchen. She stopped long enough to wash her hands. To her amusement, Daisy stayed glued to her side, endearing herself to Tracey.

"What do you think?" Roce called over his shoulder.

"The inside is nothing like the little house in the big woods I imagined. I'm impressed by what you've done with it in such a short period of time. Now, what can I do to help?"

"I made a salad if you'd like to put it on the kitchen table."

She brought over the salad and poured coffee before they sat down to eat. "Am I allowed to feed Daisy some tidbits? Her eyes are begging me."

"Only a few. I don't want her to put on weight."

Tracey fed her a little pork. "That's right, Daisy. I'll be the one who gains ten pounds tonight." Roce's eyes lit up with amusement. "This is probably one of the most scrumptious meals I've ever tasted. What kind of salad dressing is this?"

"My own version of raspberry vinaigrette."

"I need the recipe for everything."

"I'm glad you approve."

"Honestly, Roce. If you decide to change professions, you could be hired as a five-star chef."

"There's no chance of that."

She sat back in the chair, eyeing this man she was beyond crazy about already. "The way you took care of Chief let me know how much you love what you do. Did you always want to be a vet?"

He'd finished his third burrito. "The thought never occurred to me until I'd been on the rodeo circuit for a while." His features unexpectedly sobered. "After a team-roping event with Toly where we won gold buckles, I discovered that the Corriente steer had suffered an injury I'd caused. Being that I was the header, I was the one who'd done the damage."

"Oh, no."

"The look in its eyes filled me with remorse. I called for the on-site vet. He examined it and said the steer had been permanently injured. I couldn't sleep for weeks. By the end of the month I'd decided to give up the rodeo as soon as Toly could find another partner."

"You really were traumatized to walk away like that."

"I'll never forget that wounded steer. It was like it was saying, 'Why did you hurt me?'"

Roce... She could feel his pain.

"When I talked to my father about it, he urged me to put it behind me and get on with my education. By that time I'd decided to go to vet school, so I could help any animal that needed it."

Tears had filled her eyes. "I'm positive that if Chief could talk, he would tell you how grateful he is that you relieved his pain."

"Hannah would tell you he'd thank you for noticing his limp." After finishing his coffee, Roce got to his feet. "Excuse me while I let Daisy out. We'll be right back."

While he was gone, Tracey cleared the table and filled the dishwasher. The things he'd told her had touched her heart in a profound way. If she hadn't talked to John about the horse's limp, she would never have met Roce.

What would life be like if something suddenly happened and she never saw him again? She couldn't bear to think about going through pain like she'd felt when Jeff had been killed. It terrified her.

As Tracey stood at the sink, lost in her thoughts, Daisy came back inside and made a beeline for her. Roce hadn't come in yet. Filled with emotions she needed to hide, she bent to hug the dog. "What am I doing, getting this involved?" she whispered, burying her face in Daisy's silky fur.

Daisy kept trying to lick her, until Tracey lifted her head and laughed gently. "You love it here, don't you? I can see why. He's such a wonderful man, I want to be around him all the time, too. Do you want to know a secret? I wish I didn't have to leave, but I hope to come back to visit soon."

Chapter Five

Roce had come back in the kitchen, noticing the way Tracey was hugging his dog. The animal lover in her was one of the things that made her exceptional.

His dog was in heaven. There was no denying that Roce was in heaven, too. He wouldn't mind keeping Tracey here and never letting her go. His thoughts wandered to Grady who'd been on her doorstep earlier this evening.

That's when he realized others would notice when he stopped by her cabin after treating Chief. The staff cabins were too close to each other, with no trees or shrubbery separating them. Roce would attract gossip every time he pulled up and went inside. She didn't need that. The best way to be with her would be to date her away from the dude ranch.

Too bad it was getting so late. They both had to work early in the morning. He had to make a call to a rancher outside Missoula. It sounded like the man's stallion had an injured tendon and couldn't settle down.

Afterward, he would be driving to the airport to

board a jet for California. There was a veterinarian conference he needed to attend.

"Tracey?" he said to alert her he'd come back. "If you're ready to go, I'll drive you back."

She got to her feet and Daisy whined after her.

"Don't worry, you big suck. You'll see her again. I'll be home soon."

Tracey got into his truck without waiting for him. That was probably a good idea. Given the way he was feeling, Roce ached to pull her in his arms and kiss the life out of her. Instead, he started the engine and drove out to the highway.

"Thank you for dinner, Roce. I've had a wonderful evening."

"Me, too." He rounded several curves. "How would you like to go to the Bitterroot-Sapphire Animal Festival with me next Friday after work? It's being held in Hamilton."

"I've heard about that!"

"It's a fair where people show their mohair and fleece along with their sheep, goats, llamas, etc. They need vets to check the animals. We can walk around for a while, then go to dinner in town."

"How fun! I can watch you at work."

"I'm mentioning it now because I'm attending a three-day Western Veterinarian Conference in California this week. I'll be leaving from Missoula tomorrow. When I thought I would be taking care of Chief, I'd decided not to go. But under the circumstances, I'd like to hear the latest information on livestock management and equine health."

"Like what, for example?"

"It will bore you."

"Try me."

He chuckled. "Have you ever heard of EPM testing, vestibular diseases, wobbler syndrome, Cushing's equine head injuries, probiotics?"

"You mean like the probiotic snacks you bought?"

"That's one aspect."

Quiet ensued before she asked, "What will you do with Daisy while you're gone?"

"I have an agreement with Brianna that, when I have to leave overnight, she and Eli will take care of her at their house. Libby is crazy about her."

"So am I."

The closer they were to the dude ranch, the more Roce wanted to turn around and go back to the house with her for the night. He didn't like the idea that she'd have to work with Wes Hunter while he was a thousand miles away.

He gripped the steering wheel tighter. "Promise me something?"

"What is it?"

"Keep your phone on you at all times. If something comes up, I hope you'll call me. If I'm not around, my brothers are. I'll give you the ranch office number. All you'd have to do is phone and ask for Eli or Wymon. One of them would be here in a shot."

He heard her quick intake of breath. "You think there's a problem?"

Roce didn't think. He *knew*. But he didn't want to frighten her. "Don't you?"

"Maybe," she admitted in a quiet voice. "But I can always go to John."

"True. But if you're out on the trail and isolated with Wes for some reason, you could need help if he gets upset with you over something. All I ask is that you be careful and keep your cell handy."

She turned to him in the semidarkness. "What aren't you telling me?"

He'd promised John to keep the criminal information on Wes to himself. "Nothing you don't already suspect. Just that he can be quick tempered. I did learn one thing. John made it clear that Chief is *not* Wes's horse. The horses are John's property."

"I knew Wes had lied about that."

"Yup. He has anger issues and we've been caught in the crosshairs. The fact that you're the granddaughter of John's close friend, who got you a job here, makes you a target. The whole situation makes me uneasy."

"I'm pretty sure Grady is upset with me now, too."

"His jealousy of me is compounded by the fact that he feels guilty that he didn't notice Chief's limp first," Roce stated. "If Wes gives him his orders, then he's worried his job could be on the line. Don't open your door to him. I don't trust him not to do special favors for Wes to stay in his good graces."

"The whole situation is ridiculous. After constantly turning him down, I have no doubt he'd love to get me in hot water. As for Chief, even if he's brought back healthy, Wes won't let him be my mount."

"You're wise to stick with Fancy Pants, otherwise things could come to a head much sooner."

They'd reached the ranch. Roce drove straight to her cabin. After turning off the engine, he turned to her. "If you'll hand me your phone, I'll program the ranch number for you."

She did his bidding, and he soon gave it back. "On my way to Missoula, I'll let my brothers know what's going on with you. That way they'll be listening should a call come from you."

Tracey put a hand on his arm. "I can't thank you enough for watching out for me. It's been a long time since I felt this protected."

The wobble in her voice caught his attention. "Who used to do that for you?" They hadn't talked about their personal lives yet.

"My fiancé, Jeff. He was in the military. He was killed a year and a half ago while he was deployed."

Roce took a deep breath. "I'm sorry, Tracey," he whispered. "I don't know how you get over a loss like that." The revelation hit him like a kick in the gut from a bull.

"I won't lie. For the first year I don't know how I survived it. But somehow you do. And I'm here with you now, so I guess it's true that time is the great healer."

Roce pulled her against him and just held her. But their privacy was interrupted by the glare of headlights on a pickup truck driving past them and taking its time.

She lifted her head. "I wonder who that is." They both watched the truck until it eventually stopped at another cabin. The headlights went off, but it was too far away for them to see the driver.

"Does Grady drive a blue truck, Tracey?"

"No. He drives a silver Chevy Malibu." Her gaze met his. "You have a big day tomorrow and need to leave. I'm afraid I've kept you too long. Please be safe." She kissed his cheek and got out of the cab. He wouldn't have let her go, but maybe talking about her fiancé had upset her and she needed to be alone.

Once he saw the light go on in her cabin, he phoned her.

"Roce?"

"I just wanted to make sure you're all right."

"Yes. Thank you again for a lovely evening."

"I'll call you tomorrow."

"Please."

After they hung up he started his truck and drove around to get a look at the blue one. He memorized the license plate number and phoned Wymon so he could get his friend at the police department to check on it. Most likely it belonged to one of the staff, or someone visiting an employee. Roce would know soon enough.

His thoughts turned back to Tracey. He'd felt her kiss permeate his body. Since meeting her, he'd wondered how such an exciting woman was still single. The answer hadn't been what he'd expected.

Tracey had to have been devastated to lose the man she'd planned to marry. After a year and a half, she still hadn't become involved with another man or she wouldn't have moved to Hamilton for the summer.

Roce felt he'd already seen into her psyche enough to know she was the kind of woman whose love would run deep and true. Yes, he sensed her attraction to him, but after losing her fiancé, it would be another thing to hope he could fill her heart. Since her revelation, he feared his own heart was now in jeopardy.

Tread carefully with her, Clayton.

ON THURSDAY AFTERNOON, three groups of riders left the summit and descended to the Rocky Point trailhead, their starting point. Tracey rode with the Briscoe children, who were a joy to be around and had become good little riders. She'd spent ample time with them on their daily trips into the mountains.

When they'd glimpsed some deer, or a fat rabbit or a squirrel, or even an eagle, everyone had taken pictures with their cell phones, including the children. Her delight in the kids, who adored seeing the animals, was what this job was all about.

Each day that week they'd taken a different trail into the forest. When they came to a scenic area, they'd get off the horses and do a little exploring.

Today they'd ridden all the way to the spot called Rocky Point. The unusual formation of boulders, plus an abandoned sanctuary hut for the shepherds of long ago, made it a fascinating place.

After they'd taken pictures, the children wanted to dismount and explore like they always did. Tracey had started to hike with them up the incline to where there was a view. But Wes suddenly called a halt to their activity in a stern voice, telling the kids he was worried about their safety.

Tracey urged the children to get back to the horses. She wondered how their parents felt about her allowing the children to roam around, but no one had said anything. She wished Wes would have told her of his concern before they'd gone on today's ride. It was an incident she wanted to discuss with Roce.

Tonight he'd be back from the West Coast, and she had plans to be with him. They'd talked on the phone every night since he'd left, but it wasn't the same as being with him in person. He was going to pick her up for dinner and she couldn't wait.

Once she'd said good-night to the Briscoe family, she carried her gear into the tack room. Wes followed her inside. She steeled herself for an unpleasant exchange.

"We'll be getting another family with young kids from Chicago this weekend. I'm assigning them to you, but there'll be no getting off the horses when we're at Rocky Point. It's too dangerous. One of the children could start a rock slide."

"I understand." Except that she didn't. They weren't the kind of rocks that would cascade down a mountainside. Still, he was the one in charge. "I just wish I'd known before we started up there today."

"You know now." This time she didn't mistake his warning.

She was on her way out of the barn when Grady called to her, from where he was putting the horses in their stalls. "How about eating dinner with me in the ranch house tonight and we'll go for a swim after?" At this point he had to know her answer would be no.

"I'm sorry, Grady, but I have plans."

"In other words, you're not going to give me a

chance." He squinted at her. "Is it still the vet? I haven't seen him around lately."

Her patience had worn thin. "That's my business. Have a good evening."

"Sure," he muttered.

The negative atmosphere around the barn was too much. She headed straight for her cabin, angry with Wes and Grady.

What mattered was to get herself ready for Roce. Yesterday she'd driven into town after work and had bought a few outfits. Tonight she'd wear her new dark wash jeans and a filmy blue-and-white print blouse.

Roce knocked three times on her door while she was applying her lipstick. They'd decided that would be his signal. Her heart ran away with her as she hurried through the little cabin to let him in.

The sight of the tall, painfully good-looking cowboy carrying a gift basket in his arms rocked her world. While she tried to catch her breath, she noticed he wore a tan Western shirt she hadn't seen before.

"You look beautiful, Tracey."

So do you. "Thank you." She swallowed hard. "I've missed you."

"That makes two of us."

"Please come in," she said.

"This is for you." Roce put the basket on the kitchen table. She walked over to inspect the tag, which said Gifts from Davis, California. There were various fruits, gourmet items, sausage and cheese inside.

Tracey plucked a chocolate bar from the nest of goodies. "You couldn't have brought me anything I

would love more. I always want a snack after work."
She looked up at him. "One of these days I'm going to
do something nice for you."

His eyes danced. "I'll look forward to that. Are you
ready to go? I thought we'd drive to Darby and have
dinner at The Blue Joint. They serve the best fish and
chips in Montana."

"You're a fish man?"

"I'm up for anything as long as it's good."

They left the cabin and got in the truck. As they
were leaving the dude ranch, Roce glanced at her. "Did
you find out who owns that blue truck parked outside
the cabin near yours?"

"Yes. I've seen Craig Simmonds driving it. He
works in the kitchen."

"Any more trouble with Grady coming to your
door?"

"No, but he still hasn't given up asking me out. I'm
sure he'll give up soon, though. I do have a problem
with Wes I want to talk to you about."

"You mean since we spoke on the phone last night?"

She nodded.

When they reached Darby, a town of less than a
thousand people, Roce pulled up into the parking lot
of the restaurant and walked her inside. After they'd
been shown a table and had given their order, he eyed
her intently.

"I want to know what went on." Roce had a re-
assuring air of authority about him that would probably intimidate anyone not on the up and up.

Once their food arrived, Tracey launched in with an

explanation of what had happened when Wes had caught up with her in the tack room earlier. "His warning today in front of the whole group was embarrassing. It's got me wondering what else he might find fault with that will leave me looking less than professional."

Roce wiped his mouth with a napkin. "That's the point, isn't it?"

"I think so. As much as I hate to cause trouble when I've only been here six days, I'm tempted to talk to John about it. I can't do a job if I'm being sabotaged."

"Do you feel Wes is trying to get you to quit?"

She swallowed the rest of her coffee. "I honestly don't know, but my instincts are telling me yes."

"Mine are saying the same thing. He needs watching, Tracey. Be careful."

"I will. Tomorrow, I'll just play I Spy games with the children, whatever trail we take. We won't dismount. They thrive on competition. After we get back to the corral, I'll give out prizes. There'll be nothing for Wes to criticize."

"He's picked the wrong woman to drive away. You're a warrior."

Their eyes held. "I'll take that as a compliment."

"Wish I could ride with you. I already know the prize I want," he said, with a half smile that sent a thrill racing through her body.

So do I. Funny how a simple dinner had suddenly made her so breathless. "I bet Daisy is excited you're back."

"When Brianna opened the door, Daisy made a flying leap toward me that did my heart good."

Tracey could relate to the dog. "I would've liked to have seen that."

"I could hear my niece's tears all the way to my truck."

"They need a dog."

"They're planning to get one on Libby's birthday next month."

"Her first dog—what a joy!"

The waitress came over and asked if they wanted dessert. Tracey declined. Roce refused, too. He paid the bill and they left to go out to the truck.

"The last thing I want to do is take you back to the dude ranch. But you have to be up early tomorrow, and I have to stop by a client's ranch tonight to check on a horse. It could end up taking a long time. What's nice is that we're going to have tomorrow after work to be together."

She lived for every moment with him. "I've been researching the festival on the internet. It sounds like it'll be a lot of fun."

"I'll only have to put in a half a day on Saturday at the festival. If you're free, we could take in dinner and a movie after my shift."

Tracey had been hoping he'd say something like that. "Sounds wonderful."

They arrived back at the ranch way too soon. He pulled up in front of her cabin, but didn't turn off the engine. That meant he was in a hurry. Before she could open the truck door, he leaned over and kissed her temple. "Provided I don't have an emergency, I'll come by for you at five thirty tomorrow. Stay safe. You know what I mean."

"I'm afraid I do." But it was the unexpected contact that made her wish he'd given her the kind of long, deep kiss she was waiting for. "You be careful, too." She got out of the cab and hurried inside the cabin. It was getting harder and harder to leave him.

After getting ready for bed, she unwrapped another chocolate bar and took several bites before calling her family. So far she hadn't said anything about the trouble with Wes Hunter. But she did tell her mom she'd been seeing a veterinarian named Roce Clayton whose family ran the Clayton Cattle Ranch outside Stevensville.

"I've heard the Clayton name before. Isn't it a Clayton who's our state's rodeo champion?"

"Yes. That's Roce's younger brother, Toly."

"I see. Is this Roce exciting?" *Exciting* was the one-word criteria her mother used to cover a huge amount of territory.

"All that and so much more," Tracey confessed, as her gaze lit on the basket of goodies he'd brought back from California. How could she explain the most incredible man she'd ever met?

The second that thought filled her mind, she realized she really had moved on from past pain. It had happened so fast, she couldn't believe it.

"That's what I've been hoping to hear one day."

"I'm feeling guilty. You don't think it's too soon to feel like this again?"

"You can't measure the speed of a relationship if it's

right. There have been other men you've dated since Jeff with no sparks. But I can tell this one has already lit up your world. How marvelous for you. Go with your feelings. A second chance to find true happiness is what I want for you."

"I love you, Mom. I'll call you on Sunday morning when I'm off work, and tell you more. Give my love to the family."

Tracey clicked off, then brushed her teeth before climbing into bed. Once nestled beneath the covers, she went over every minute of her evening with Roce.

You're a warrior.

She'd never thought of herself like that. The way he'd said it made her think it was a good thing in his eyes. Hopefully, more than a good thing. She wanted to be the one he'd been waiting for.

Chapter Six

Roce drove home at midnight after taking care of a horse that had been kicked in the mouth and had lost some teeth. Once he'd seen to Daisy's needs, he went into his office to check his answering machine. Most patients left a message there, but if it was an emergency, they could contact him on his private cell phone.

To his surprise there were a dozen calls, one from the organizer for the animal festival, verifying Roce's participation. Another came from Hannah's daughter, who had some medical instruments from her mother he might like.

Two others came from an old client, Marcie Hewitt. He'd taken care of her cat and had gone to dinner with her after she'd insisted, in order to show her appreciation. The evening hadn't gone anywhere and she knew it. But it looked like she needed to hear the words, something he didn't want to have to do. He put off calling her back, since he assumed this call had nothing to do with the health of her cat.

Eight calls came from clients, five of them new. He

had his work cut out for him tomorrow. Word was getting around that he had relocated.

The news was encouraging, but it made him realize he was going to need a receptionist if this continued, in order not to lose business. Tomorrow he'd look into a job service in Missoula. There were people out there applying for receptionist jobs. If he was lucky he'd find one who'd worked for a veterinarian before. It would make their job easier.

Roce also had a text from Wymon, telling him that the blue truck he'd asked about was registered to a Gil Pilchovsky from Arlee, Montana. Maybe this Gil had allowed Craig Simmonds to borrow it. But he saw no link to Wes Hunter.

Roce texted back his thanks and went to bed with his thoughts on Tracey. He worried how far he should take this relationship with her. There were other women he could date—Marcie excluded—in order to protect himself from being hurt. If Tracey started giving off signals that no man could replace the fiancé she'd lost, he didn't think he could deal with it.

But no matter how hard he tried, he awoke early Friday morning with her on his mind. Around noon, his phone rang while he was pumping a dog's stomach because it had eaten too many chocolate chips. The owner had been baking and the bag had fallen on the floor. Her bichon had lapped them up so quickly she couldn't stop him in time.

After seeing them to the door after the procedure, and assuring the woman her dog would be fine, he checked his phone. The text message from Tracey said: Call me, please.

His adrenaline kicked in as he pressed the button to reach her.

"Oh, Roce. Please forgive me for bothering you. I'm so glad you phoned." She spoke in a whisper. "We're out on the trail. Wes is up in front with his group. You won't believe it. He's riding Chief!"

Roce sucked in his breath.

"I can't believe he brought him back from Darby and is making him work. It's way too soon!"

"You're right. Do you notice any limping?"

"No, but the children and I are bringing up the rear, so I can't keep a good eye on him. Rod's and Colette's groups are in front of me. I know you can't do anything about this. Neither can I. But I'm so outraged, I had to call you."

He was grateful that she'd turned to him. "I'm glad you did. No doubt Chief is still in pain, but there's nothing we can do about it right now. Don't do anything to antagonize Wes. Promise me you won't say anything."

"I promise."

"Good. When I pick you up after work, we'll talk about how to tell John. It will be up to him to act."

"Wes has a cruel streak. The horse could still go lame."

Unfortunately, there was so much more that she didn't know. "You'd better get off the phone before he catches you talking."

"You're right. Thanks for listening. See you tonight."

The click resonated in his heart.

Roce worked solidly until a quarter to five. Brianna came by and took Daisy home with her for the weekend. Relieved he didn't have to worry about his dog, he showered and dressed in jeans and a plaid shirt.

For once, he didn't phone Tracey. He simply showed up at her cabin at five-thirty. But he didn't have to knock, because she stood outside waiting for him, in jeans and a red cotton sweater that molded to her body and did wonders for him. She ran and opened the truck door, bringing her flowery scent with her.

"I've been waiting for you." She acted so eager to see him, it gave him hope she was letting go of past pain. Trying to tamp down his emotions, he squeezed her hand instead of devouring her in plain sight.

They took off for the Hamilton fairgrounds. "I'll be on call until ten tonight, but we're free to walk anywhere we want." He drove to the tent where he had to check in. "Give me a minute to get my tag. Then we'll get something to eat."

After he'd gotten squared away, he jumped back in the cab and they drove to the concession area, where they bought Pronto Pup deep-fried hot dogs and frozen yogurt swirls on a stick.

Tracey took a bite. "The smell of these takes me back years to other fairs and rodeos."

"I know what you mean." They got back in the truck, where they could eat and talk in private. "Now tell me what happened on the ride after you called me."

Tracey's features sobered. "Once we arrived back at the trailhead, I tried not to look at Wes at all. When we reached the corral, I said goodbye to the Briscoe family, then put my gear in the tack room. On the way out, I noticed Wes had put Chief in his stall. I just kept walking, but I felt his gaze on my back. I know he was waiting for me to say something, but I took your advice."

"I'm glad you did," Roce said.

"That poor horse shouldn't have to put any weight on his foot yet."

"Agreed." Roce pulled out his cell phone. "I'm going to call John and ask him to meet us in town this evening, away from the ranch. If he agrees, then we'll tell him everything that's happened since the day you arrived from Polson. That way Wes won't have any idea what's going on."

She nodded. "That's the best plan. I hope you can reach him."

He put in a call, but had to leave a message. "I'm sure he'll call me back at some point. Let's walk over to look at the angora goats first. They're beautiful and they'll make you laugh out loud."

"Why?"

"Because they live in a herd and have a distinct social pecking order. You'll see them gang up on each other on a regular basis."

She chuckled. "I had no idea."

For the next hour they walked around the pens holding various breeds of sheep and goats. A couple goats had pushed their heads through the fencing. Roce stood behind Tracey with his hands on her shoulders.

"See those two?" he murmured into her silky hair.

She nodded. "They'll stay there until they can push all the way through. They don't know how to reverse themselves."

She turned to him with a smile. "You mean they won't budge?"

"Nope. Someone will have to help them. I guess that's up to me. Come on."

Tracey followed him and watched as he extricated their heads and gave them a push. Her full-bodied laughter told him coming here and enjoying the animals had taken away her concerns for a little while.

She oohed and ahhed over the fleece and mohair for sale. The handmade clothing and accessories, as well as the decorative art displays, brought the crowds. Tracey particularly liked the quilts made of textiles, and bought one for her mother. While she appeared engrossed in the weavers' activities, Roce talked with the animal stewards to learn if there were any problems that needed a vet's attention. So far, no red flags had been raised.

At a quarter to eight, John phoned him back. Relieved to hear from him, Roce indicated that he and Tracey needed to talk to him about something important. Would he be willing to meet them at the Pine Cone in town? It was a bistro that stayed open past eight, where they could order hors d'oeuvres and drinks or coffee without having to consume a full meal.

After he hung up, he looked at Tracey. "He'll meet us ASAP. Let me return my tag. I'm still on call until ten, but they can phone me at the bistro if an emergency crops up."

"I hope we're doing the right thing."

His jaw tautened. "Your safety is more important than anything else, Tracey."

Her eyes searched his. "I can tell you think Wes is a real threat."

"So do you," he replied.

"You're right. I'm glad we're going to talk to John. He needs to know what's going on."

TRACEY'S TRUST IN Roce had become absolute. She didn't know how she knew it, but she did. If he was worried enough about her for them to go to John, then the situation was potentially serious. When the older man had hired her as a favor to her grandfather, who would ever have imagined this happening?

"What's going on in your mind?" Roce asked, getting into the truck after signing out for the night.

"I'm crushed by all of this. I don't know if I told you—John had made arrangements for a vase of flowers to be put in my room that first day to welcome me to the ranch. His card was very sweet. Because my grandfather had confided to him about Jeff, he said he hoped that being here would help me get over my sadness." Tears stung her eyes. "John is a wonderful man. He doesn't deserve this."

They headed to town. "Life isn't always fair. He shouldn't have to worry about a grandson who's making life miserable for Chief, let alone intimidating you."

"Something's very wrong with him."

"Don't worry. I'm sure John will get to the crux of the problem."

It didn't take long to reach the Pine Cone. But being a Friday night with crowds from the festival, they had to park a block away. Roce threaded his fingers through hers and kept her close to him as they walked to the bistro. Tracey noticed how many women looked at him as they passed. She felt a ridiculous sense of pride that he wanted to be with her.

No sooner did they go inside than they saw John, who'd beaten them there. They were shown to a table and a waiter brought them coffee and appetizers. The older man sat back in his chair and eyed both of them with a worried expression.

"Sheldon and I had Hunter Oil business meetings in town today. You caught me before I could drive back to the ranch to pick up Sylvia and take us both home. The timing is perfect. Tell me what's wrong."

Tracey flashed Roce a silent message before sitting forward. "I've been discussing all this with Dr. Clayton and we decided we had to talk to you. In order to tell you everything, I need to start at the beginning. I'm so sorry, but this is about your grandson Wes."

John nodded, not acting in the least surprised. "Go on."

"Could I ask you a question about him first? Is he Grady Cox's boss?"

"No. I'm the one who hired Grady three years ago for summer work. His job is to take care of the horses and he reports to me. Wes helps in the stable and co-ordinates the trail rides. He, as well as all the employees, including my children and other grandchildren, answer to me, no one else."

"That's interesting. When you told me I could look over the horses and pick the one I wanted, I chose Chief. But Grady told me Chief was Wes's horse. Wes told me the same thing the next day."

The older man's brow furrowed. "There's no truth to it. He has to ride one of the horses in the barn like everyone else. Wes doesn't own one."

"I didn't think so. Otherwise you would have told me ahead of time. As you know, when I could tell Chief was limping and said he needed a vet immediately, Grady was caught off guard, because he hadn't noticed it. I could tell he was nervous about it because he had no way to consult Wes, who'd gone into town and hadn't returned yet."

"You think Grady was afraid of retaliation?"

Tracey looked at Roce before answering. "I don't know, but it seemed like he was under Wes's thumb. On Sunday morning, when I asked Wes about choosing a horse I could ride, he told me he'd already picked one out for me—a mare named Fancy Pants. He figured I'd be able to handle her."

John looked aggrieved. "I'm very sorry to hear this. That mare is meant for people who've never ridden a horse before."

She flashed him a brief smile. "I thought so."

"You should have come to me sooner."

"I didn't feel it was my place. Grady appeared to know all about it and told me the mare was a nice, docile horse. I couldn't tell if he was trying to convince me because he thought I was an inexperienced rider, or if Wes had told him to tell me as much to put me in my place."

"Wes had no right—"

"I'm sure it upset your grandson that I suggested you call Dr. Clayton to look at Chief's hoof. It's clear he feels I'm his enemy."

Roce nodded. "I'm afraid we're both the enemy, John."

He leaned forward to stare at Tracey. "What else do I need to know?"

She took a deep breath. "On Monday morning he assigned the Briscoe family to me. They have two young children. I loved working with them this week. Every time we'd go out on a trail ride, I tried to make it extra fun for them.

"One thing they loved to do was take pictures along the route for souvenirs of the trip. But on our last trail ride, we rode to Rocky Point and I let the children dismount so they could explore the area.

"Suddenly, Wes warned us to get back on the horses. He claimed we could start a rock slide and it would be dangerous, but those boulders aren't the kind to come falling down on everyone. Still, we did what he said.

"When we got back to the corral I asked him to please warn me before the ride next time, so I didn't do anything else wrong. It was embarrassing. I don't want the people I'm in charge of to think I don't know what I'm doing."

John shook his head. She knew this information was hurting him, but he needed to hear it all.

"I'm afraid that when he assigns me the next group,

he'll find something else about me he doesn't like. But you haven't heard the thing that concerns me the most. Today he was riding Chief."

"What?"

Roce nodded. "No one should ride that horse until his hoof has healed. He needed at least a two-week recovery. I'm sure Dr. Cruz would have told your grandson the same thing. In my opinion, Wes brought the horse out early and rode it today to cause a reaction in Tracey."

"What are you saying?"

Tracey broke in. "I think he hopes I'll quit and leave the dude ranch."

John sat immobile for a minute, then pushed himself away from the table and stood up. "The last thing I want is to lose you, Tracey. Don't you worry any more. I'm going to take care of everything." He put some bills on the table.

"Dr. Clayton? If I could talk to you alone for a moment?"

"Of course."

"I'll be right back," Roce whispered near her ear. His warm breath on her skin sent tingles down her spine. He was gone only a few minutes before he returned and walked her outside to the truck. She could tell he was deep in thought.

"What's wrong?"

"After we get back to your cabin, I'm coming inside and we'll talk." He was still trying to compose his thoughts.

"Is it something serious?"

"Yes, but I don't want you to be nervous."

"All along you've known something you haven't shared with me, and that's why you've been so protective."

He took her hand in his. "I can see why Wes doesn't want you around. Your instincts are right on and have spooked him."

"You were speaking the truth when you said we were both Wes's enemies," Tracey murmured.

"None of it matters now that we've been honest with John."

Thankful as she was that the three of them had talked, she knew more was coming and feared it wouldn't be pleasant. Once they got back to the ranch, she found her eyes straying to the corral and barn, wondering if Wes or Grady were still around. But everything looked quiet.

It was dark by the time Roce parked in front of her cabin and they both got out. Tracey didn't care if the presence of his truck would cause everyone to gossip. She needed him with her tonight, and unlocked the front door.

"The bathroom is through there if you want to freshen up."

"Thanks."

While he disappeared, she went over to the kitchen sink and washed her hands. It didn't escape her that Roce had come in the cabin for a specific reason. But oh, how she hoped he wanted to be alone with her for a reason that had nothing to do with Wes Hunter.

Being with Roce in his truck or walking around

wasn't enough. She wanted to know what it felt like to be enveloped in his arms and kissed until she couldn't breathe.

THE MAN STARING back at Roce in the mirror wasn't the same person who'd answered a medical emergency at the dude ranch last Saturday. That man had been getting through each day working without respite. Though he'd been focused on his career during the recent renovations to his house, he'd wondered when or if he would ever find the kind of love enjoyed by his married brothers.

This evening he didn't recognize himself because of the beautiful woman in the other room. Just thinking about her caused his heart to race in his chest. Even before meeting her for the first time, he'd liked the sound of her voice. One look into those violet eyes had burned into his psyche like a brand meant to last forever.

When he walked into the living room, he discovered her on the couch. She was just getting off the phone. Something was wrong.

"Are you all right?" Roce asked.

"Yes, but I don't quite know what to think. Fran left me a message telling me I wouldn't be needed for the Saturday trail ride tomorrow, so I get the whole day off."

Roce sank down on a chair near her. "Sounds like John has already taken charge of the situation by removing you from any trouble."

"What trouble, Roce? Please tell me what you know."

He sat forward with his hands on his thighs. "Last Sunday, John asked me to come to his office. When I told him what was going on with Wes, he confided some unsettling information to me. I would have told you everything, but he asked me to keep it to myself so you wouldn't be alarmed."

"So why are telling me all this now?"

"Because tonight he gave me permission. Wes had some DUIs in college and three months ago he was arrested for horse theft."

"No way."

"John had hoped his grandson was turning his life around, but nothing could be further from the truth. My brother Wymon checked with his friend on the police force. It turns out Wes has a record, but the details of his arrest are sealed. John knows all about it and realized he couldn't keep you in the dark after what you told him this evening."

For the next few minutes Roce told her what John had worked out with the court for Wes—that he was allowing him to do his community service on the ranch without pay for the summer. His wife, Fran, was the only one earning a salary right now.

Tracey shot to her feet. "How could he not be grateful to his grandfather? Otherwise he'd be doing jail time."

"That's not all," Roce told her. "When his service is over, he'll have to get a job and earn the five thousand dollars he owes his father for paying off his fine, plus the cost of a new truck and trailer."

She shook her head.

"He was ordered to go to counseling by the court, but in my opinion he needs more intensive psychotherapy. He obviously hasn't learned a thing from his mistakes."

"This is incredible, Roce. I wouldn't be surprised if he has a personality disorder of some kind. The psychologist at my school has talked to me about a few students who display similar behavior. They're not difficult all the time, but something triggers a reaction and they become unreasonable."

"Sounds like Wes. My concern is that he's planning something illegal right under his father's and grandfather's nose."

"You mean maybe stealing the horses his father buys for the ranch?"

"Possibly, or someone else's. He could sell them and make a big profit. I think your unexpected arrival at the ranch has thrown a roadblock in his plans. John agrees with me."

"I'm sure you're right, Roce. He wants to get rid of me so I won't catch on to his plan to steal his grandfather's other horses. I wonder if Grady knows that and is trying to run interference by getting me to go out with him. Maybe Wes hasn't wanted his wife to help on the rides so she won't see anything that's going on."

"Maybe." Roce watched her pace the carpet and wanted to reassure her. "I have no doubt that John has talked with Sheldon and they've already taken steps to deal with Wes tonight. What's important here is that you don't have to report for work until Monday morning."

"I know." She swung around. "You don't know how relieved I am!"

Roce stood up. "It fits in with my plans for us, if you're willing."

"We're already spending time tomorrow at the festival."

"And maybe dinner and a movie after," he said. "But I'm talking about Sunday, too. That's my free day. I'm hoping you'll spend the whole day with me. We could go riding in the Sapphires and take a picnic."

"I'd love that more than anything."

Before he could reach for her and show her how he felt, his phone rang. The interruption had come at the wrong moment.

She smiled at him. "Better answer it, Dr. Clayton."

Roce checked the caller ID. To his surprise it was John. He picked up. "Mr. Hunter?"

"Glad you answered. Sheldon has found a place in the area where Wes can continue with his community service. It's been cleared by the attorney. He won't be coming back here."

Thank heaven.

"After a talk with Dr. Cruz, who knows about Wes's history involving his own son, he understands why I won't be using his services any longer. As of now, I'm retaining you as our ranch's new vet, if you're interested."

The news overjoyed Roce for several reasons. "I'd be honored."

"You've relieved my worries. Would it be possible for you to check on Chief tonight? He's in his stall. If you're already home, though, you can check on him in the morning."

Roce eyed the woman who'd transformed his life. "I haven't left the ranch yet. I'll drive over to the barn now."

"That's wonderful. I've had a chat with Grady and he's been reminded that he answers to me. He's been told Wes is gone for good, and he'll meet you at the barn. I want him to be on hand for any help you need."

"I appreciate that."

"Is Tracey with you?"

"Yes."

"May I speak to her?"

"Here she is." Roce handed her the phone.

"Hello, John?"

"Tracey—I'm sorry I didn't tell you about Wes sooner. Blame an old man for expecting the best from his own grandson. Thank you for coming to me with the truth. Wes needs help and he's going to get it. Just know our ranch needs you to be part of our staff and help on the trail rides."

"Thank you. That means everything to me."

"Mr. Briscoe told me you made such an impression with his children that they didn't want to leave. They've already booked another stay with us for next summer."

"I'm so happy to hear that."

Roce saw tears in her eyes.

"Repeat business is vital for us. I'm so proud of you and will tell your grandfather the next time we talk. Good night."

"Good night." She hung up and handed the phone back to Roce. "What did he say to you?"

"He told me that Wes is gone for good and he'd like me to be the dude ranch's vet."

"Roce—that's fantastic!"

"I know." He smiled at her. "And you're the reason for that. He asked me if I could go check on Chief right now." The last thing he wanted to do was leave, but he didn't have a choice. "John told Grady to be there to help me. Much as I'd like you to come with me, I think this time—"

"It would be better if you go alone and establish a professional relationship with him," she said.

"Thank you for understanding. I'll be back early in the morning to check on Chief before I have to report in at the festival. I should be through my shift by two, then I'll come pick you up. We'll have the rest of the weekend to do whatever we want, as long as I don't have any emergencies."

He needed to get out of there. But at the last second he obeyed a desire he could no longer put off and pulled her into his arms, tasting her luscious mouth for the first time.

Roce had been dreaming about this moment and was overwhelmed by her response. She was kissing him back as if her life depended on it. As if there was no ghost between them. How he wished that were true.

"See you tomorrow," he whispered, before leaving the cabin.

Chapter Seven

Tracey touched her mouth with her fingers. What she'd wanted to happen *had* happened. The hunger in his kiss had set her on fire.

We'll have the rest of the weekend to do whatever we want.

She knew what *she* wanted. Roce had just been made the new vet of the Rocky Point Dude Ranch. He'd be coming by all summer for legitimate reasons. They'd be together on a regular basis.

To add to her happiness, John had made her feel wanted and welcome. And now Wes was gone...

She was so excited she knew she wouldn't be able to sleep. After getting ready for bed, she plucked an apple from the gift basket and lay down on the couch with a quilt to watch TV.

At eleven thirty she received a text from Roce.

I knew you'd want a report. Chief is in pain. I've soaked his foot, put on a poultice and started more antibiotics. We'll have to wait and see if he has survived this without further damage. Looking forward to tomorrow.

Tracy hugged the phone to her heart. *So am I, Roce.* She turned off the TV and went to bed, needing to-morrow to come.

When morning arrived, she awakened early and was tempted to walk over to the barn to see him when he drove up. But she checked that impulse. He hadn't asked her to meet him at the barn. Now that she thought about it, he hadn't asked her to join him at the festi-val, either.

There had to be a reason. It hurt that maybe it meant he wasn't that into her even though his kiss had implied otherwise. She needed to face the facts. Roce was still single, but there must have been so many women over the years who'd hoped to become *the* one.

Just because he'd kissed her didn't necessarily mean anything serious. Naturally, he'd kissed a lot of women. But one kiss from him wasn't enough for her. She wanted more and knew she would be in a perma-nent state of aching for him. Tracey had never thought of herself as a needy person, but that was the way she'd been feeling since he'd come into her life.

Deep down she had to be honest with herself. She knew that no matter how long she looked, she'd never meet another man like Dr. Rocelin Clayton. Her mom had talked about her getting a second chance at hap-piness. She was right. Tracey had fallen in love with Roce and no one else would ever measure up.

She stayed in bed and listened to the radio while she daydreamed about him. Eventually she got up and showered and dressed. Since she was hungry, she decided to drive into town for breakfast and to stop at a Laundromat.

Tracey could eat at the ranch house and do her laundry there, too, but she'd been given the day off. The last thing she wanted was to talk to anyone and have to explain why she wasn't working today.

She grabbed her laundry bag and detergent, and left for town. At the drive-through, she bought a breakfast burrito and a hot chocolate, then headed for the Laundromat. As soon as she'd started her wash, she took a seat to wait. But before she could pull out her Kindle, Craig Simmonds approached her carrying a laundry basket.

"Tracey Marcroft. How did I know this was the place I would finally find you?"

Craig was the one who drove the blue truck and worked in the kitchen. He had cute dimples and was probably college-aged, too. "I didn't know you were looking for me," she said teasingly.

"You're the now-you-see-her-now-you-don't woman. You're hardly ever around at meals and never in the swimming pool. What's a guy have to do to spend time with the best-looking woman this side of the continental divide?"

The guy had a line ten miles long, but she didn't mind. "Only the continental divide? I think I'm insulted."

He laughed. "I can see I have my work cut out for me. The other evening I saw you with another guy outside your cabin." That explained the headlights she and Roce had both noticed. "Is he someone special, or would you be willing to go out with me sometime? Deanna Hunter is my boss, and she'll vouch for me that I'm a nice guy."

Craig was nice, but she decided she'd better be honest. "If I weren't involved with someone else, I'd say yes."

He looked disappointed. "Grady told me I didn't have a chance against the vet who showed up last week. Is he the one?"

There was no point in denying it. "Yes."

"Well, you can't blame a man for trying."

"Of course not. I'm sorry, but you made my day with your compliment."

He put a hand over his heart. "I'm afraid that doesn't help me none."

She chuckled. "Your turn is coming."

"You think?"

"She might be the next person who shows up at the dude ranch. You never know what will happen when you get up in the morning."

"So far, not much has."

"Don't give up." Tracey had driven past the Clayton Veterinary Hospital never imagining that the vet who owned it would change her entire life within hours of her arriving at the dude ranch.

He nodded. "I'll be here for a while. See you back at the ranch."

"Absolutely. Bye for now, Craig."

When her laundry was done, she left for the ranch to shower and wash her hair. Roce had told her he'd be by after he finished his festival work around two.

Several hours and a phone call from her brother later, Tracey put on her makeup and fastened her leaf-green earrings. She was just putting on her sandals when she received a text from Roce.

I finished my shift early to deal with a patient. Now I'm home and have to return some calls from patients. Would you be willing to drive to my house? We'll make plans after you get here.

Relieved to hear from him, Tracey congratulated herself that she hadn't tried to crowd him earlier. She texted back that she was ready and would come now. She flew out the door wearing skinny jeans and a new summery green-and-white-print swing top.

Clouds had moved in over the mountains. There might even be a storm before evening. Tracey didn't care as she left the ranch and headed for Roce's home. In fact, she couldn't imagine anything more wonderful than being alone with him.

She pulled into the parking area next to the house and got out of the car. She braced herself for a welcome from his dog, but when Roce answered the door, she didn't see her. Their gazes fused. He was so painfully handsome, Tracey couldn't think for a minute. "Where's Daisy?"

"Sorry, but she's at Libby's house. Is she the reason you came?" he asked.

Warmth filled her cheeks. "Daisy's one of them." After the door closed she gasped, because he'd grasped her waist from behind. With her back pressed against his chest, he buried his face in her hair.

"After that kiss last night, I've been counting the minutes until you got here." His lips grazed her neck before he turned her around. "I don't know about you, but this is what I've been waiting for since the first time I laid eyes on you."

His mouth descended, closing hungrily over hers in a deep, voluptuous kiss like the one he'd given her last night. She'd been dying to be with him like this again. Since meeting him a week ago, her need for him had grown so great all it had taken was this taste of him for her passion to catch fire and never go out.

Clasped against his hard body, she found herself trying to get closer. His hands moved over her arms and back, shaping her to him as they sought to become one. If it weren't for the ringing of his cell phone, Tracey had no idea how long it would have taken for them to break apart. She moaned in protest before remembering he was a doctor and some animal in trouble needed him.

Still clinging to her, he tore his lips from hers to answer it. As time went on, emotion darkened his eyes while he listened to the person on the other end. She couldn't imagine what was wrong, but whoever had phoned was telling him something that had taken him away from her. He let her ease out of his arms.

Tracey stood there waiting for him to finish the call. When he rang off, he put his arm around her shoulders and walked her into the kitchen. "I have something important to tell you. Let's talk over lunch. I never did have mine."

He made ham sandwiches and poured them coffee. They sat at the table to eat.

"After I left you last night, I had a conference call with my brothers. We devised a plan to keep an eye on what's going on with Wes." The news surprised her. "I know John loves his grandson and hopes his son Sheldon can handle the situation now that he's found him another place to do his community service. But I'm not so sure it's that simple."

"John is too trusting."

"I think so, too." Roce finished his sandwich and poured a second cup of coffee. "Frankly, I don't have any idea how wide a net Wes Hunter has thrown over some of the employees working on the ranch. He had accomplices when he stole that horse. We know he intimidated Grady and could still plan to stay in touch with him and others for personal reasons, no matter where he's been placed."

"But he's under court order, so what are you saying?"

"Just this. In my opinion, what he did by being abusive to you and Chief was criminal, but not in the eyes of the law. Wes didn't commit a crime against his grandfather by taking Chief without permission or riding him when he wasn't well.

"Here's the point. He's still free to function the way he wants as long as he puts in his community hours. But being a loose cannon with a personality disorder, as you have suggested, he's capable of causing more harm and using his friends to help him."

"You're right."

"I'm glad you recognize it. I know in my gut that when John chastised his grandson for treating you the way he did, and hurting Chief, those words will have fueled Wes's anger against you. Though he has to work off his hours at another nearby location, it won't stop him from doing more damage when the day is over. I don't trust him."

"Neither do I."

"That's why Wymon followed me to the ranch early this morning in his car and kept a watch on your car until you drove into town."

"Your brother was here?"

He nodded. "We thought Grady might be keeping tabs on you per Wes's orders. Instead, my brother found out that Craig Simmonds followed you to the Laundromat in the truck he doesn't own."

Aghast, Tracey got up from the table. "I thought it was odd he showed up there. We all do our laundry at the ranch house. For obvious reasons I decided not to go near it today."

"Did Simmonds talk to you?"

She nodded. "He flirted with me and mentioned seeing me with another man outside the cabin earlier in the week."

"That was the night when those headlights were focused on us."

"Definitely. He asked me to go out on a date. When I told him I was seeing someone exclusively, he indicated that he knew it was the vet. I told him yes, so he'd get the message."

Roce's jaw hardened. "Simmonds was spying for Wes. No doubt he's already reported your conversation to Wes himself, or to Grady, who will pass it on. When I take you back to your cabin tonight, we'll check on Chief first. After I leave the dude ranch, Eli will be there to keep an eye on you throughout the night. I'd do it, but I have to drive out to the Holgren ranch to do what I can for their very sick brood mare."

Tracey shook her head. "I'm not your problem."

He got to his feet and put the dishes in the sink. "We've been in this together since that first night. As for my brothers, you have to understand we help each other."

"But they shouldn't have to do this for me. I can't let them. They have families of their own. I'm afraid that if anyone is a target, it's you."

He leaned against the counter. "I can take care of myself. My concern is for you. Even though I know how grateful you are to John, if there's another incident that could put you in jeopardy, I'm hoping you'll tell him you can't work there anymore."

She rubbed her arms. "I couldn't do that to him."

"Not even if you know you're in danger?" he demanded in a controlled voice.

Tracey bit her lip. "You honestly think it could come to that?"

"You and I got in the way of Wes's plans and he was exposed. It's my gut feeling that after his first horse theft was thwarted, he was planning to steal Chief and sell him."

"Of course," she agreed.

"But when you noticed the limp, it changed everything. He's not going to let this go. Wes hasn't gone to jail for his cruelty to Chief, but I'm convinced it's only a matter of time before he's in trouble again."

"I'm going to have a little talk with Fran and find out what she knows."

"That could be tricky."

"When I first came, she told me to come by if I ever needed someone to listen. Maybe I can return the favor."

"Maybe." Roce walked over and put his hands on Tracey's shoulders. "Just remember what Wes is capable of. Look what he's done to his grandfather even after John worked out that first deal with the judge. Think of the pain he's caused Chief, John's best and favorite horse."

"It's all I've been able to think about."

His hands cupped her face. "I've been thinking of what a jerk he's been to you."

"I guess it's time to talk to my grandfather."

"That's a good idea. I'm sure he'd tell you to leave the dude ranch at any more signs of trouble."

He probably would, but it would mean leaving Roce. She couldn't bear the thought. "I'd need to find another summer job."

"That could never be a problem for you." Roce pressed an ardent kiss to her mouth. "You need cheering up. Let's get out of here and go to a movie in town."

She wanted to curl up in his arms and finish what they'd started. But the specter of Wes Hunter had loomed too large to throw off. To realize that she was being watched and followed had shaken her to the core.

"I'm so lucky I met you, Roce." She gave him another kiss before he walked her out to his truck.

ROCE HADN'T LIKED putting Tracey on her guard, but she needed to be aware of what she was up against. After the film, which turned out to be an uninspiring dark comedy, they went to dinner at Marie's for a home-cooked Italian meal.

"Shall we get back to the ranch and take a look at Chief?"

"Please. I'm anxious to see if his hoof is any better."

Darkness had fallen by the time he drove them back to the house in his truck. "I'll follow you. Give me a minute to load the radiography machine so I can take X-rays."

Once that was done, he helped her into her car. "It's starting to rain. Drive safely and remember I'm right behind you." Unable to stop himself, he kissed her long and hard before shutting the door. Once behind the wheel of his truck, he phoned Eli to let him know they were headed to Hamilton.

"I'm on your tail, bro. What's the latest news?"

"Craig Simmonds and Grady Cox are both spying for Wes Hunter." Roce talked to his brother about Tracey's conversation with Simmonds in the Laundromat. "I wish to hell we knew where Wes's father took him last night."

"That would help. We'll just have to figure out another way to track him down."

"Tracey's going to talk to Fran. Maybe we'll learn something. Be sure to tell Wymon what I found out."

"I will. Right now he's working with a detective to learn what he can about the guy who owns the truck Simmonds is driving."

"I can't thank you guys enough."

"Forget it. It's our pleasure."

Roce hung up and phoned Tracey. "When we reach the dude ranch, drive straight to the barn. We'll go in together. I'm going to need you to help steady Chief while I take the X-rays. If Grady is around, just act as normal as you can."

"Don't worry."

To his surprise he saw Sheldon Hunter on the premises when they pulled up outside the barn. Roce turned off the windshield wipers. The rain was coming down hard. There was no sign of Grady.

Tracey got out of her car and hurried over to carry his doctor bag while he took in the portable X-ray equipment.

Sheldon waited for them outside Chief's stall. "Dad told me he has hired you to be our official vet. Welcome aboard. I'm glad you're here. Chief needs attention." He turned to Tracey. "For the time being I'll be in charge of the trail rides. You can choose whatever horse you'd like on Monday morning."

"Thanks, Mr. Hunter."

"Both of you call me Sheldon."

Everyone avoided the mention of Wes as Roce

brushed the raindrops off his bag and opened it. While Sheldon got him a bucket of warm water, Roce unwrapped the poultice. There'd been more drainage, which meant the hoof wasn't free of infection yet.

Following that, he set everything up to remove Chief's shoe before he took an X-ray. He asked Tracey to hand him the hoof rasp and clippers from his bag. After ten minutes the shoe came off and he filed down the clinches.

"Now we'll take a picture from half a dozen angles and find out if there's been some serious damage done."

Tracey patted Chief's neck and spoke in gentle tones while Roce worked. When he was ready, he told her how to hold the plate. She made a great assistant. Before long he finished up and then soaked the hoof in more warm water and Epsom salts. Lastly he applied a fresh poultice.

"I'll take a look at these pictures back at the hospital and we'll see what else might have to be done."

Those fantastic violet eyes beseeched him. "What do you really think?"

"I don't like the way Chief is favoring his leg. His pain has affected his whole stance. My gut tells me he'll probably go lame, but I'll do everything I can to prevent it."

Tears glistened on the ends of Tracey's eyelashes. She was so beautiful he wanted to pull her into his arms, but he still hadn't finished taking care of the horse.

Reaching into his bag, he drew out the balling gun

with the antibiotic and helped Chief swallow it. "There you go, buddy. We're going to get you better."

"We are," Tracey cooed with her arms around his neck.

Sheldon eyed the two of them. "I'll empty the bucket and tend to Chief. My son should never have brought him back from Darby this early."

"Well, he's getting the help he needs now," Roce said. He gathered up his equipment. "Come on, Tracey. I'll follow you to your cabin."

They said good-night to Sheldon and went outside. The rain had turned to a drizzle. Roce followed her in his truck, keeping an eye out for Simmonds or Grady. He purposely drove past Simmonds's cabin, but the blue truck wasn't there.

Tracey held the cabin door open. He walked inside and headed to the kitchen to wash his hands and arms. She brought him a towel. Roce thanked her. "You're a terrific helper, you know that?" He studied her for a minute. "How would you like a job with the newest vet on the block?"

Her eyes lit up in amusement. "You mean helping you while you X-ray your patients?"

His mouth curved. "That and other things, like answering the phone, making appointments. The money wouldn't be great at first, but there would be insurance *and* perks."

"Really?" she drawled. "What kind?"

"Besides taking care of Daisy when I'm out on calls, you'd live at the family ranch house and have your own horse to ride whenever you want."

"This sounds like a genuine job offer."

"A temporary one for as long as you need to stay away from the dude ranch." He folded the towel and put it on the counter. "When I left the hospital in Missoula, I knew I'd need an assistant. That time has come. Before I start advertising for one, I thought I'd let you know about it in case you were interested. Another scare from Wes is one too many."

Her expression sobered before she absently rubbed her hands over her hips. "You're serious."

"I wouldn't have mentioned it otherwise. Why don't you think about it?"

She turned and went into the living room. He trailed her. Tracey wheeled around, looking stunned. "I couldn't live at your family's ranch house. I wouldn't dream of imposing on your family like that."

He raised an eyebrow. "A lot of people have lived there at one time or other for indefinite periods, including the woman Wymon married. My mother has to put business people up all the time who need to stay over. We have a housekeeper, Solana, who'd take care of you."

"If the improbable happened and I did decide to work for you, I would find a place in Stevensville to live."

"But you wouldn't be on Clayton land, where you'd be protected. It's a two-minute drive from the ranch house to mine."

She lifted her head and the lamplight made her silvery-gold hair appear to glow. "When you do hire someone, will you tell them they can live in your mother's home?"

"No."

"Why not?"

"Because they won't be Wes Hunter's target."

She averted her eyes, making Roce wonder if he was moving too fast for her, especially if she wasn't completely over the death of her fiancé.

"Tell you what. I'll be by at seven thirty in the morning to check on Chief. Afterward, we'll eat breakfast on the way to the ranch. Depending on the weather, I'll ask Solana to fix us a picnic and we'll take a long ride in the mountains. I want you to see where I grew up."

His phone rang, interrupting them. He checked the caller ID. "I've got to go, Tracey. Are we set for tomorrow?"

It took a few seconds before she said yes. Roce knew she hadn't been expecting a job offer from him. It was too big a decision after what she'd lived through.

"Good." In a few swift strides he reached for her and kissed her fully on the mouth before leaving the cabin.

As soon as he climbed in the cab, he returned Eli's call. "What's up?"

"Five minutes ago Simmonds drove in to the ranch. He dropped another man off in front of the barn before going to his cabin."

"It was probably Grady. The pot has been stirred." Roce turned on the engine and headed toward the highway. "Grady's going to find Wes's father inside and learn I was there to take care of Chief."

"I'll keep an eye on both men tonight. Tomorrow

morning, Wymon will take over for me. We're going to hunt Wes down and discover what he's up to."

"I take it Wymon doesn't have any new information yet."

"Not yet. But he will."

"You two are the best. I'm headed home. I've asked Tracey to spend the day with me on the ranch tomorrow."

"Nice."

Nice didn't cover it and both men knew it. In all these years, and all the women Roce had dated, he'd never brought one back to the ranch. He was in so deep with Tracey, he'd already offered her a job. Until he felt she'd accept a marriage proposal, he'd do whatever it took to keep her close and safe.

Geez. Has it only been a week?

Chapter Eight

Sunday morning turned out bright and clear. The storm had moved on, ensuring a beautiful day in the mountains. Though tempted to talk to her grandfather about Wes Hunter and the situation, Tracey put it off, because Roce's job offer had really thrown her.

She was crazy in love with him, yet he wanted her to *work* for him. It wasn't that she didn't appreciate his trying to help her out of a potentially dangerous situation. But she didn't want to be his assistant. She'd hoped he couldn't live without her, either, and wanted her for his wife one day!

Was there something wrong with her, to love him this much after just one week? Did it mean she wasn't over the pain of her dreams being shattered a year and a half ago? A psychiatrist would probably tell her she needed therapy before making a decision that could bring on more pain.

If it became clear she was in more danger, she could give John her notice and return home to Polson. But that would allow Roce to hire someone else—probably a lovely young woman who would fall in love with him on sight. Neither alternative was acceptable.

Roce, Roce.

Tracey showered and dressed in jeans and a Western shirt. With her makeup applied and her hair brushed, she put her phone in her pants' pocket. After pulling on her cowboy boots, she donned her Stetson and left the cabin for the barn.

She could see Roce's truck in the distance. The sight of it caused her breath to catch. Anything to do with him had the same effect on her.

No sooner had she reached the barn than Wes's wife approached her, the very person she'd wanted to talk to. "Hi!" Fran's smile seemed forced. Tracey couldn't imagine how hard this had to be for her.

"Hi, yourself. It's nice to see you."

"John told me I'd probably find you here. Since you haven't been to the ranch house for a few days, he asked me to come out here and give you this present from the Briscoe family." She handed her a small, gift-wrapped box.

"What a surprise! Thank you."

"You're welcome. See you later."

"Wait, Fran." She hurried after her. "I'm so sorry for what has happened. John told me Wes has found another job somewhere else. That must be so hard on you to be separated from him during the day."

"But we're together at night."

"Of course. Are you going to continue working here?"

She nodded. "For the time being."

"Where did he go?"

"To a farm outside Hamilton."

"Oh, good. Then he's close."

"Yes. He has to be."

"I'm sure he wants to be near you."

"I hope so, but he's been getting therapy for a drinking problem he's tried to overcome for several years. He can't miss his sessions."

"I'm sorry you're going through such a tough situation right now."

"So am I. Thanks for caring."

"Of course. See you later."

After Fran ran off, Tracey walked into the barn and found Sheldon with Roce, who was already soaking Chief's hoof again. He looked up and their eyes held. "Good morning. What have you got there?"

"A gift from the family I rode with all last week."

"Aren't you going to open it?"

Tracey smiled and undid the wrapping. Inside the box was a set of silver cowgirl earrings with a dangling bronco rider charm. "How sweet. Their daughter loved my earrings. These had to have been her idea."

"You made a big hit."

She put them back in the box and tucked it in her back pocket. "How's Chief?"

"His hoof is still draining, but not as badly."

"That's good."

"I'll apply a poultice and give him another pill, then we can leave."

"What did the X-rays show?"

"He has a fracture that extends up the midline of the bone into the coffin joint."

She frowned. "Coffin joint?"

"The fracture is deep inside, like a body in a coffin. In time he'll be able to handle light riding and going out to pasture, but he's lame. I fear there'll be an onset of osteoarthritis as a result of the damage from the fracture."

"It's a damn shame," Sheldon muttered.

Roce looked up at him. "I'll send for the farrier to apply a bar shoe to the hoof. It will protect the rim. In the meantime, if you'll supply some deep bedding, it will help pad Chief's hoof and induce him to lie down. We'll keep him in the stall and comfortable until he's recovered."

Sheldon nodded. "I'll take care of it." He removed the bucket and left to empty it. Tracey carried Roce's vet bag out to the truck and climbed in.

He soon joined her and they left the dude ranch. "Where would you like to eat?"

"Why don't you let me do something nice for you? If you'll stop at the grocery store, I'll pick out the items I need to make us breakfast."

Roce flashed her a smile. "You're on."

Within forty-five minutes they'd reached his house and she'd put the ingredients together for French crepes, one of her specialties. Roce ate half a dozen, along with a half pound of bacon cooked crisply, the way he liked it. When they couldn't eat another bite, she told him to relax while she loaded the dishwasher. "Remember. This is my treat."

He watched her from the kitchen table. "Those crepes are my new favorite breakfast. What was the secret flavor?"

She chuckled. "Spoken like a five-star chef. After cooking them, you spread on orange juice and powdered sugar before rolling them up."

"The citrus. That was it!" He got up from the table. "If you opened up a little French crepe shop here in Stevensville, you'd become a millionaire overnight."

Tracey darted him a covert glance. "First a vet assistant, now a chef. Are you trying to tell me my efforts are being wasted on the dude ranch?"

He moved closer and cupped her face in his hands. "Are you really surprised?"

But before she could answer, his phone rang. They were both frustrated by the interruption. Roce pressed his forehead against hers before he checked the caller ID and clicked on. It sounded to her like he was talking to one of his brothers.

After hanging up, he said, "Wymon is on his way back from the dude ranch. He wanted us to know he did surveillance early this morning. Both Simmonds and Grady met at the barn before I arrived."

She moaned. "There was no reason for Craig to be there. He's supposed to be helping in the kitchen with the meals."

"Wymon found out something else even more important. His friend at the police department phoned to tell him that the owner of that blue truck has just reported it stolen."

She stared at him. "You mean since he checked the criminal database the first time?"

"Yes. It just came in. Wonders never cease, do they?"

She shook her head. "That means—"

"The police are looking for it," he stated, breaking in. "And *we* know where it is. I have to alert John, who will have to call the detective working on Wes's case and tell him everything we've learned."

"This is terrible, Roce." She sat down on one of the chairs. "If you hadn't told Wymon, and he hadn't called his friend, we wouldn't know how far-reaching this is. Craig told me he started working here last summer. It looks as though two troubled souls found each other," she confided.

"Or they'd joined forces long before Craig applied for the job. Wes probably arranged it. John has unloaded to me. Because he's a very wealthy man, Wes feels he's entitled to everything. He doesn't think his grandfather is being fair.

"We talked about Grady and believe maybe he helped Wes steal that horse three months ago. For that matter, John is wondering if there are others working on the ranch who are tied up with Wes. It's clear John no longer trusts Grady."

"To think Wes could do this to his grandfather and family is beyond heartbreaking. Poor Fran. She told me Wes is working on a farm near Hamilton."

"That's important information!"

"She also said he's going to therapy for a drinking problem."

"At least that's what she's been told." His features hardened. "What I can't forgive is his lying to you and criticizing you." The ice in his voice caused Tracey to shiver. "Excuse me while I call John."

For the next ten minutes she listened while Roce talked to him. When she became the topic of conversation, it didn't surprise her, but her pulse sped up to think her job could be on the line because of the precariousness of the situation.

Once again Roce handed her his phone. "John wants to talk to you."

She nodded and said hello.

"The news Dr. Clayton has just given me forces me to make a decision I don't want to make, but it's for your best interest, Tracey. I would never forgive myself if anything happened to you under my roof. Therefore, I'm asking you to leave the dude ranch today for at least one week, maybe two, while the police investigate everything."

Her eyes closed tightly.

"Please don't be concerned. You'll be paid whether you are here or not. But it's imperative you don't step foot on the property until the threat is over. I told Ben you would be safe with me and I have to keep that promise."

"I understand." Her voice caught.

"Your cabin will be waiting for you when you return. Take the things you need before you leave."

"May I ask one favor?" she requested. "Will you let me tell my grandfather?"

"Whatever you want, Tracey."

"Thank you."

"Goodbye for now. We'll stay in close touch." She heard the click and handed Roce back his phone. "He told me to leave the ranch ASAP."

"Thank God."

"But what about you?" she said, getting to her feet. "You're as much of a target as I am. I don't care if you're the new vet. You should stay far away, too."

"Let's not worry about that right now. John is calling the detective as we speak and will get back to us when he has more information. Since it's Sunday and I have the day off, we're going to go on that horseback ride and enjoy the picnic Solana is preparing. We'll worry about getting your things later. Give me a minute to check my messages in the office first." He brushed his mouth against hers before leaving the kitchen.

Tracey gripped the back of the chair, mentally rehashing the conversation she'd just had with John. He'd relieved her of her duties for a couple weeks. Now Roce was acting as if it was of no consequence because she could stay with his family.

But she wasn't his responsibility!

What she needed to do was ask him to drive her back to the dude ranch. She would pack up and leave for Polson until it was safe to return. The thought of moving away from Roce caused her so much pain she could hardly breathe, but there was no way she would allow him to take care of her. Tracey didn't have the right and the situation wasn't of his making.

A few minutes later Roce returned. "Are you ready to go?"

She took a deep breath. "Yes, but if you don't mind, I'd like it if you would take me to the dude ranch and wait while I pack up my stuff. As much as I'd love to go horseback riding with you today, I'll have to give it a miss and go back home for a while."

Lines suddenly darkened his features. Tracey would like to think it was because he didn't want her to go, but they'd known each other for only a week. It was too much to hope that he'd fallen in love with her. A miracle like that just didn't happen.

"There's no need for that. You've got a job here with me, starting today."

Since there'd been trouble with Wes, Roce had invented the job, realizing she might need a place to go for protection. From the beginning she'd sensed intrinsically that he was the heroic kind of man who was a breed apart from everyone else.

But she wasn't born yesterday. He'd barely gotten his new hospital started and wasn't ready to hire anyone yet. Though there was nothing she'd love more than to stay here and lean on him, she refused to be one of those lovesick, pathetic, desperate women.

"I can't thank you enough for the offer. It's so generous, but my mind is made up. I'm just glad I could cook you breakfast after all the things you've done for me." Without waiting for a response, she hurried through the house to his truck and climbed into the cab.

He eventually joined her and they took off for the dude ranch. "You're wrong if you think I manufactured the job for you."

"Even if I am, I have to leave. John has already said

he doesn't want me anywhere near the ranch. If you knew my grandfather, you'd understand that when I tell him about this, he won't rest until I'm home. Do you think I'm happy knowing you're going to stay on as John's vet? We have no idea what danger is lurking right now."

"You're jumping to a lot of conclusions, Tracey."

"But the threat is real and you know it, otherwise John wouldn't have decided to let me go. So don't tell me I'm overreacting."

Roce didn't argue with her. Instead he grasped her hand for the rest of the drive.

The proliferation of cars around the ranch house that Sunday afternoon meant the new groups of tourists had arrived. Roce drove past them to the cabins beyond the corral and pulled up next to her car. "Let's do this fast and get your things packed. Maybe we can get out of here before one of Wes's spies sees us."

She could only hope. "It won't take me long."

They hurried inside. She pulled her suitcases out of the closet and got busy. With Roce's help the job took only half the time it would have normally On the last trip outside, she carried the gift basket of half-eaten goodies he'd given her.

He helped her get in. "I'll follow you to my house. I want to have a final meal with you before you drive all the way home."

A final meal. She felt as if she was going down for the third time.

TRACEY THOUGHT SHE was going home to Polson, but Roce had news for her. As they drove away from the dude ranch, he phoned Eli to alert him about the latest events. Luckily, it was Sunday and the family was home. After telling him his plans for Tracey, he asked him to bring Daisy to the house when he could.

Eli assured him the dog would be there waiting for them. Roce clicked off and phoned Wymon to convey the same information. "John has told her not to come back for a couple of weeks. She thinks she's going home."

He heard Wymon's deep chuckle. "Things couldn't be working out more perfectly for you."

"Except that she already turned me down when I offered her a job with me." That was probably because she didn't want to make any kind of a commitment to him. If she was still in love with the memory of her fiancé, it would explain her determination to return to Polson.

"If I know my brother, you'll do something she won't be able to resist."

"I'm working on it." But how did you fight a ghost, if that was the real reason she was so hell-bent on leaving?

"Good luck, Roce, but watch your back."

"I hear you." They clicked off.

While he kept his eyes on the rearview mirror, wondering who might be following them, he phoned Solana to let her know the picnic had to be canceled.

After thanking her for going to the trouble, he told her to surprise her husband, Luis, with it and go off on a romantic getaway. Her warm laughter told him she might just act on his suggestion.

He breathed a sigh of relief when Tracey pulled into the parking lot next to the house. Roce drew up beside her and helped her out of the car. Already he could hear Daisy barking inside.

Tracey eyed him in surprise. "She's back?"

"Eli returned her. He said she's been missing me."

"Oh…the little darling."

He pulled out the remote that operated the electronic lock. Daisy flew through the air and ran rings around both of them. She was so excited that she jumped up to kiss Tracey, sending her into a fit of laughter.

"I've missed you, too. Did you have fun with Libby?" She burrowed her face in the dog's fur and led her inside.

Roce shut the door, loving the way they interacted. "She might need to go out again. If you want, open the back door for her."

"Come on, Daisy." She put her down and they headed for the kitchen. If Roce didn't know how attached the dog was to him, he could've been hurt that Daisy would transfer her allegiance so easily. But Tracey wasn't just any person. She had a sweetness and love for animals that shone through, and Daisy sensed it.

He went to his office to check his messages. Glad to learn there were no emergencies, he walked back to the kitchen and filled Daisy's dishes with food and fresh water.

With that taken care of, he started cooking hamburgers and got out the ingredients for another green salad. While he filled a bowl with potato chips, Tracey came back in. His dog rushed over to him. Roce played with her, then let her go so she could drink.

"Daisy is adorable."

"She thinks you are, too," he murmured. "Come and sit down. Our food is about ready."

"Let me just wash my hands. I'll be right back."

Like clockwork, Daisy followed her down the hall to the bathroom. He could hear Tracey's gentle laughter. The joyful sounds of the two interacting were like music to his ears.

A deep feeling of contentment seeped through him. After a lifetime of searching, he felt she was the missing piece of a difficult puzzle, a piece that had finally turned up. Until now, he'd never been able to finish it. There was no way he would allow her to leave him unless she told him she was still too heartbroken over her loss to truly love another man.

"Oh, boy, Daisy, hamburgers!" Tracey sat down before flashing Roce a glance. "Maybe I can prevail on your doctor and master to give you part of one." Her fabulous eyes, a lavender-blue at the moment, melted him on the spot.

He poured coffee for them and sat down. "It's possible...but comes at a steep price."

"Ooh. That sounds a little scary." But she said it with a smile and they began to eat. After a minute she served herself some more chips and said, "How steep?"

It pleased him that she hadn't been able to let it go. "Be with me until John asks you to go back to the dude ranch."

She stopped chewing. "I told you before. I couldn't do that, Roce."

"I'm not talking about you staying at the main ranch house at night, or renting a place in town. I want you here with me all the time, where I can protect you. There's a perfectly good bedroom down the hall I won't invade. Mine is upstairs. We'll treat my house like a hotel. Since I need someone here to help me, it's a perfect solution and will keep you busy while we wait to hear from John."

"Except that it wouldn't work."

"Why not? It would only be for a temporary period."

To his surprise, she got up from the chair. "For one thing, I don't want to be your assistant. I'm a schoolteacher. That's what I'm trained for. If I go back to Polson, I might be able to fill in at a summer school."

She'd just administered a gut punch. "In that case, just be my guest and accept my hospitality. Wes Hunter has put both of us in a difficult situation, but this makes the most sense. If the police settle this matter sooner, you could be back at the ranch in another week."

"What if it goes on much longer?"

"What if it does?"

"Stop it, Roce! You know I can't accept your offer."

"Because you're not that kind of woman? Don't you think I know who you are?"

"That isn't what I meant," she said. "But it doesn't matter."

"It does to me. Tell me why you're fighting me so hard on this. Don't you agree we've become good friends?"

"Of course."

"You trust me? Like me?"

"That's not the point."

"Then what is?"

She shook her head. "I have to go. Thank you for the lunch. I can't tell you how much I appreciate all the things you've done for me, but I can't go on taking from you forever."

"You've taken nothing I haven't wanted to give."

A moan escaped her lips. "There's no winning an argument with you."

"That's what my brothers tell me," he said. "Why the big hurry to leave? It won't take you that long to drive home."

"I'd rather not drag this out any longer."

Roce got to his feet. "Drag what out? I thought we were having a leisurely Sunday meal. Are you that anxious to get back to Polson?"

"As a matter of fact, I am."

"Did you call to tell your parents you were coming?"

"No. I'll phone them on the way."

"Then there's no hurry. Why not stay with me a bit longer? Daisy will be devastated when you go."

"You're the one she worships. She'll get over it."

"But *I* won't," Roce said.

Her head lifted. "What do you mean?"

"Have you considered how much I'm going to miss you when you're gone? I've gotten used to being with you. When I visit Chief, it will be strange to realize you're so far away."

"Don't forget that cute waitress in Hamilton who's

dying for you to come in again. I bet she'd love to be your assistant if you offered her the job."

Tracey started through the house to the front door.

He followed her. "There's just one problem with that," he said.

She looked over her shoulder at him. "What would that be?"

"I'm in love with *you*, Tracey Marcroft. Not anyone else."

Roce heard her sharp intake of breath. She fell back against the door, as if she couldn't believe what she'd heard.

"Just so you know, if you walk out of here now, it means you don't feel the same way about me. How could you when your heart is too full of your love for the fiancé you lost? I'll have to handle that. But you need to know I won't try to see you again, because it will hurt too much."

"Roce..." He could see her trembling. "You know how I feel about you. You *know* it."

"I do?"

"Do you honestly think I could have spent this whole week with you, kissing you, talking to you, laying my life wide open to you, if I weren't ready to love you with all my heart and soul? Jeff will always have a special place inside me, but he's gone and life is still ahead of me with you."

"Then come here and show me."

She flew to him faster than his dog ever could. With an exultant cry, Roce drew her into his arms and swung her around before carrying her down the hall to the bedroom. He closed the door so Daisy couldn't come in, then followed her down on the bed with his body and proceeded to devour her.

For the next while they both forgot the world in their need to express feelings they'd kept in check until now. She gave him kiss for kiss until it all melted into one explosion of rapture. There were no words to express the way this fabulous woman made him feel.

"I love you so much," she whispered feverishly, covering his face with kisses. "I fell instantly in love with you. It was like a dream. What I can't fathom is that you love me back. We only met a week ago. It's too soon to feel this strongly."

"Who says it is, or cares?" He buried his face in her neck. After kissing her senseless, he lifted his head. "I knew how I felt that first evening when I saw you standing next to John. My breath caught because the late afternoon sun had turned your hair a flaming silvery-gold. I still have that reaction every time I see you.

"Do you know your eyes are the color of larkspurs? I want to ride with you in the mountains and show them to you. I want you in my world, Tracey. I couldn't handle the thought of you leaving."

Her heart streamed into her eyes. "I don't want to leave. And I didn't mean what I said about not wanting to be your assistant. You know I didn't. There's nothing I'd love more than to help you any way I can."

He looked down at her, smoothing her hair away so he could kiss every inch of her face. "Then it's settled. While I go out to the car to bring in your bags, why don't you call your family? Tell them how we got involved in the first place and that I've asked you to stay here until the police say it's safe to go back to the dude ranch."

She clutched his arms. "If you're sure."

"I've never been so sure of anything in my life."

She returned his kiss, answering him with the kind of fire that sealed his fate. How he'd managed to live all this time before meeting her he couldn't comprehend. All he knew was that the long drought was over and a life filled with this woman's love was beginning.

Chapter Nine

Tracey woke up the following Sunday morning no longer knowing herself. After living with Roce in his house for a glorious week, she felt as if she'd arrived in heaven, but feared it couldn't last. They'd made no promises and hadn't slept together yet. She knew he was trying to honor her, because he was that kind of man, and she adored him for it.

Her mom and dad had shown great understanding when she'd explained about Wes and everything that had happened. As for her grandfather, he'd sounded grateful she was living under Roce's protection.

When Roce wasn't out on a call or with a patient in the surgery, they cooked, cleaned, had long conversations, took Daisy for walks, laughed, watched TV and held each other. Every night it got harder to say good-night and disappear into their individual bedrooms. The times when he did have to leave, the dog was her constant companion, and Tracey had never been so happy.

So far they hadn't heard from John. Roce hadn't seen him when he'd driven to the dude ranch in the mornings to check on Chief. He was thrilled with the horse's improvement and chatted with Sheldon about giving Chief light exercise. But the other man had shed no news about his son and Roce hadn't pushed him. All was quiet in that department.

Tracey was beginning to think the first week of her stay at the dude ranch with Wes on her case had been a bad dream. In her heart of hearts she was ecstatic that she didn't have to go back there yet. Every time she answered the landline phone at the house, she looked to see if John's name showed up on the caller ID. When it turned out to be a patient or one of Roce's family members, she let out a sigh of relief.

Today, after he returned from checking on Chief, they were going on a long ride in the mountains—the one they'd planned to take last Sunday. This time *she* insisted on fixing them their picnic lunch, which she would pack in a saddlebag. While she was wrapping their roast beef sandwiches, Daisy started barking.

"I know. Roce's home!" Her heart skipped a beat. The dog barked louder than usual. Tracey had never seen her so worked up. "Just a minute and I'll let you out." She washed her hands and hurried through the house to open the door so Daisy could run to greet him. *Devoted* wasn't the word.

The second she unlocked it, the dog shot outside. Tracey expected to see Roce's truck, but he was nowhere in sight. Daisy kept running around her car. "What's wrong?" She walked closer, knowing she kept it locked. Nothing looked disturbed inside. Maybe an animal had been creeping around. She hoped not a skunk.

"Come here, Daisy." She hunkered down and held out her hand. That's when Tracey saw that her tires were flat. "What?" She got up and ran around to the other side of the car. The other two tires looked like pancakes. Four tires didn't lose every bit of air at the same time without help.

Angry heat crept into her face as she realized the culprit must have been outside the house five minutes ago. Daisy was a great little watchdog and had heard someone out here.

Which one of Wes's friends had been sent to vandalize her car? Or was it Wes himself? Had they done any other damage?

Tracey ran out to the highway to see if she could see a familiar truck or car driving away. Several vehicles drove by in both directions, but whoever had done the deed had made a quick escape. She called Daisy to follow her and went back to the front porch.

Grabbing her phone out of her pocket, she dialed Roce. He answered on the second ring. "Tracey? I promise I'm on my way home."

"Thank God."

"What's the matter?"

When she told him, he said, "I'm calling the sheriff. Either he or one of his patrols will be at the house shortly. Go inside and stay locked in. I'll be home before you know it." He clicked off so fast she couldn't get in another word.

Tracey went in and watched for him from the living

room window. Daisy never left her side. Before long she saw Roce drive up. He leaped from the cab and started inspecting the tires of her car. She rushed over to open the door, and Daisy raced toward him. Roce looked up at her. His grim face said it all.

"They've been slashed. At least no glass was broken to get inside your car. I called my brothers, who were at Mom's for lunch. They're on their way over. Once the police are through here, I'm phoning John so he can get in touch with the detective."

When Tracey walked up to him, he put his arm around her and hugged her close. "I'm sorry I wasn't here when this happened."

"We know that's why it was done. Someone has been watching the house and waiting until you were away."

After he'd given her a kiss that didn't last long enough, a police car pulled into the parking area, followed by the sheriff's car. Behind it came another truck.

"Good. My brothers are here, too." Roce let her go and put Daisy back in the house. She didn't like having the door closed on her.

The barrel-chested sheriff got out and walked up to them.

"Sheriff Garson?"

"That's right. You're Dr. Clayton?"

"Yes. This is Tracey Marcroft, who was hired by John Hunter. These are my brothers, Eli and Wymon Clayton."

He nodded to them. "We've met at different times.

I've had several talks with John, who's just in agony over this ugly situation. Tell me what's happened here."

While the officers went over her car and dusted for fingerprints, Tracey told him what had happened while she'd been in the kitchen. "I'm just worried that there might be other vandalism besides the car."

"I'll ask the officers to check around the house's exterior. They'll dust for fingerprints at all the windows and doors, too."

"It's obvious someone who knows Tracey's car was watching when I left for the dude ranch," Roce interjected. "That's when they came around. After your men are finished and can give Tracey a report for the insurance, I'll run into town and get new tires for her car. But from here on out we'll keep it with the other cars outside my family's ranch house when it's not in use," Roce asserted.

"Good idea. I'm glad you're all here. We need to talk. Will it be all right to go inside?"

"Of course." Roce ushered them into the house and asked everyone to sit down in the waiting room. Tracey had never met the Clayton brothers, who were both very attractive. As they took turns reporting what they knew, they exhibited the same authoritative demeanor as Roce.

The sheriff spoke to Wymon. "Thanks to you, your friend at the criminal records division gave us our first real break in this case. I'm now free to reveal the details. The owner of the truck that Craig Simmonds has been driving is Gil Pilchovsky. He's a member of the artist guild in Arlee, Montana, and had stored his truck in a warehouse. Only last week did he discover it had been stolen.

"After that knowledge was fed to the detective working Wes Hunter's case, Simmonds was finally arrested—the night before last."

"Thank goodness," Tracey muttered.

"Right now the detective is working on a plan to tie Craig Simmonds, Ramon Cruz and Grady Cox to the horse theft that led to Wes Hunter's arrest. Thanks to both Wymon and Eli and their surveillance activities at the dude ranch, we now have new information that Mr. Cox was not behaving on the up-and-up."

Tracey eyed the sheriff. "Roce suspected something wasn't right with him."

"You Claytons have all the right instincts. The detective did some more investigating and discovered that Cox had produced a false résumé to the Hunter family when he sought employment. It's been learned that Mr. Cox is not a student at Montana State and was never registered."

Tracey gasped.

"He's lived on and off with a group of male friends in Conner and has tended bar at several locations in the past to earn money."

"They've all lied!" she cried. "Wes probably told him to make up that business about college to impress his grandfather."

"Afraid so. As soon as the detective went to John with the news, he fired Cox. Told him the police have been informed of what he did. Since they're already thinking he might have been in on the horse theft, he'd better be careful."

Daisy climbed up on the sofa beside Tracey. She hugged her. "It's unbelievable that Wes could allow his family and grandfather to be used like this, let alone abuse his grandfather's horse."

Roce sat forward. "I'm thinking he planned to steal John's best horse, Chief, in order to sell him and pay back the five thousand he owes his father, so he can get out from under his thumb. What he didn't count on was Tracey noticing the limp and getting in the way of his plan.

"If Sheldon hadn't stepped in to pay that fine in the first place, Wes would have gone to jail. It's where he should be. We found out through Fran Hunter that he's doing his community service somewhere else now," Roce added.

The sheriff nodded. "His father found him work on the Skipper fruit farm, between Hamilton and Darby."

"Fran is happy he's still close."

"Sheldon wanted it that way, to keep an eye on him. A father doesn't want to give up on his son. I'm afraid this case is far from over. Mr. Hunter has hired body-guards to keep him and his family safe, but he's worried about you and Dr. Clayton. After the damage done to your car, you must take all the precautions you can in order to protect yourself."

"Don't worry," Roce stated, in the most forbidding voice she'd ever heard. "No one will hurt Tracey. I'll see to it."

"We'll all see to it," his brothers echoed.

"The forensics report on your car will be sent to the detective. Perhaps there'll be a match that provides a link to the case. Ms. Marcroft? If you'll come outside, we'll see if the officers have finished their business."

Tracey went with him and signed the report. They gave her a copy and the three men left. When she turned around, Roce was there to wrap his arms around her.

"Simmonds is now in custody, and Grady has been put on notice. Knowing the police are watching him, he's likely not anxious to get into any more trouble right now, I wouldn't think. That leaves Wes and Ramon. One of those thugs could have slashed your tires. Let's go in and plan a strategy with my brothers."

Once inside, Roce pulled Tracey down on the couch next to him. Eli had been holding Daisy, but let her go now that the door was closed. She nestled in beside Tracey again, warming her heart.

Eli grinned. "My daughter would be so jealous."

"I hear she's getting a new puppy on her birthday."

"That's the plan. Since we haven't been introduced, I'll do the honors. I'm Eli. And this is our big brother, Wymon."

Roce clasped her hand. "Sorry, Tracey. I lost my manners. I'm afraid my mind has been somewhere else."

"So has mine. It's wonderful to meet both of you. I'm very grateful for all you've done to help us."

Wymon sat back in his chair with a smile. "Didn't Roce tell you we're the Four Musketeers? 'All for one, one for all,' that sort of thing. Toly's here in spirit."

Tracey chuckled, liking his family so much already. The three of them had no right to be so handsome, along with everything else.

"Who do you think slashed the tires, Roce?"

He shook his head at Eli. "I don't know. It could be one of Wes's toadies that we have no idea about."

"That's what I'm thinking," Wymon murmured. "An unknown who could show up outside your house with no one the wiser."

Eli tried to get the dog to go to him, with no luck. "You have to assume the detective has run a check of everyone associated with the ranch. What about Wes's wife? It's amazing how loyal some spouses can be to a man with a criminal background."

"I can't see Fran doing something so terrible." Tracey looked at Roce. "She was so friendly and kind to me when I first arrived. Remember the day she ran out to the barn with the gift left by the Briscoe family, and we talked?"

Roce nodded. "She seemed nervous that day, right?"

"She did. She's probably trying to hang on to her marriage. Given Wes's temper and drinking problem, she likely feels she has to be careful not to make a misstep."

Wymon got to his feet. "Tracey? If it's all right with you, Eli and I will buy you a new set of tires in town and be back to put them on."

"I can't let you do that. It's too much trouble for you."

"We want to do it," Eli declared.

"Then let me give you a check."

"Let them do it," Roce whispered. "Go on, guys. When you get back you can enjoy our picnic with us. If I know Tracey, she's made enough food for a dozen people."

"That sounds about right, since she has to keep you fed."

Eli laughed at Wymon's joke and they left the house.

Tracey kissed Roce's jaw. "They're wonderful."

"That's what they think about you."

"You don't know that."

"I could tell by the way they were looking at you. It's something you can't hide. I know *I* can't." He pushed her back gently on the couch and started kissing her.

The taste and feel of him set her on fire. For a little while she was able to forget the ugliness of what had happened earlier, and gave in to her hunger for him. But their euphoria didn't last long. The telephone had a way of interfering at crucial moments. It was driving her crazy.

Roce let out a groan before sitting up to answer it. After a short conversation, she heard him thank Eli before he hung up.

"Only a few tire stores were open and none of them have your size. We'll have to check with one of them tomorrow. That means you're stuck and we'll have to get along with my truck. I told my brothers to go home to their families."

"I'm glad you did. They've done more than enough and put their own lives at risk. Roce, I'm worried. You can't tell me Wes and his cronies don't have weapons."

"I'm sure they do. That's why we're going to pack you up and take you to the ranch house until this over."

"No, Roce. Moving me there threatens the safety of your whole family. I won't do it. Either I stay with you, or I'm going home as soon as I can get new tires on the car. Hopefully, I'll be able to leave some time tomorrow."

He stood up. "Be reasonable, Tracey. Our foreman, Luis, will help me organize some of the hands to take turns supplying extra security."

"But who will protect you in this house?" she demanded, and got to her feet.

"I'm going to hire a private detective to do surveillance."

"That's too expensive."

"Not really. Let me worry about it."

"You don't need to hire anyone. I can handle a rifle and a pistol. Our family has done a lot of hunting. If Wes or one of his thugs tries to break in to your house, I'll be ready for him. All you have to do is lend me one of your guns, maybe?"

THOUGH IT THRILLED Roce that she was fighting to stay here with him, his fear that he could lose her was playing havoc with his judgment.

"I don't doubt you know how to shoot a gun, but under the circumstances, I can't let you stay here alone during the times I'm gone. Since you won't go to the ranch house, I might as well drive you to Polson now. When your car is ready, I'll get one of my brothers to follow me to your parents' home so I can return it."

A hurt look crossed over her beautiful face. "Why do I get the feeling you're glad this has happened?"

"What in the name of heaven are you talking about?"

"Even though we've both admitted we've fallen in love, maybe too much togetherness has gotten to you. I was afraid this would happen. You haven't been a bachelor all these years for nothing."

He shook his head. "I haven't lived like one since I met you. I've never asked a woman to live with me. Doesn't that tell you anything?"

She bowed her head. "I don't know what it means, except that I was too eager to move in with you and now you're anxious for me to leave. Since you haven't tried to make love to me, it makes it much easier to—"

"You know why I haven't," he interrupted.

"I do, actually. You're a man who's been taught to honor a woman."

"Would you rather I didn't?"

"No, Roce." She half moaned the words. "I mean—that's not what I meant."

"Then help me understand."

"I don't think I can." Her voice faltered.

"Try."

"All I'm saying is that we both got carried away with our emotions. I made a mistake by moving in here so fast after only knowing you for a week. I'm horrified to think that my being here has provided Wes with a double target. But since we've been living together these last seven days with no strings, it's the perfect time for me to leave. Surely you have to know that I'm indebted to you for everything you've done."

"It's gratifying that you feel that way, but I'm not hearing anything close to the truth."

He could hear her shallow breathing. "I need to put the sandwiches in the fridge before we leave." She started for the kitchen.

"Since you've made them, I'm ready for a late lunch." With Daisy at his heels, he followed her and walked over to the counter to unwrap one. He ate it in a few bites and reached for another sandwich. "These are delicious. What's that flavor?"

"An avocado dressing with minced lemongrass."

"Fantastic."

"Please don't say I could open up my own deli."

"I wouldn't dream of it. For your information I have a much better job in mind."

"I'd rather not hear it."

"Then I'll let this speak for me."

He pulled out the ring that had burned a hole in his pocket since she'd agreed to live with him. Reaching for her left hand, he slid it home on her ring finger.

Roce leaned against the counter while he waited for a reaction. It took a long time to come. She moved her finger this way and that so the dazzling gemstone would catch the light.

The sapphire shop his mother owned and ran farther up the mountain was a Clayton family legacy. He'd been up there to see his mom the week before and had asked her to show him the violet sapphires mined on their property.

Her smile had said it all. She'd worried about him for so long. Now his secret was out. After giving him a huge hug, she'd poured some gemstones from one of her many pouches onto the velvet runner. The second he'd spied the two-carat sapphire, he could see Tracey's eyes in its color and had asked his mother to set it in a medium-width white-gold band.

Except for the thud of his heart and Daisy's begging sounds, quiet reigned in the kitchen. He fed the dog part of a sandwich to keep her quiet.

"How long have you had this?" Tracey's tremulous voice revealed the depth of her shock.

"I bought it from my mother last week while I was checking on one of the calves."

Tracey turned to look at him, clearly confused and mystified. "Your mother?"

"It's obvious you don't know the story about the Sapphire Mountains. They've yielded around one hundred and eighty million carats of sapphire over the last hundred plus years. Some of the fractured stones used for industry ended up in Switzerland for watch bearings.

"Right after World War II, people starting digging for them. Our family brought sapphire gravel out of the mine on our property and opened the Clayton gem shop. Some people still try to find an uncut gem on their own, but most prefer to visit the shop my mother owns and see the sapphires on display."

"I had no idea," Tracey murmured.

"Being her children, my brothers and I have always been fascinated with what came out of the mountain.

Eli gave Brianna a blue sapphire in a heart shape for their engagement because she was born on Valentine's Day. My big brother followed with a spring-green sapphire solitaire when he asked Jasmine to marry him. Both of them chose gems that matched their wives' eyes.

"If you look in a mirror, you'll see that your eyes match the color of the stone you're wearing. I happen to like the princess cut. I didn't know the name of it until Mother educated me. It's very fitting for you, since you look like a princess."

Those gorgeous eyes filled with tears. "You want to marry me?" Her words came out more like a squeak.

"Do you honestly think I would have asked you to live with me if marriage hadn't been on my mind all along? I would have given this ring to you last week, but I was afraid you'd reject me so fast, I'd never have a chance with you."

She looked haunted. "You didn't know what was going on inside of me."

"How could I? You don't ask a woman who recently lost her fiancé to marry you within a week of meeting her. The way I felt about you *did* happen too fast. I was terrified you'd never feel the same way. My heart almost gave out when you told me you wouldn't stay at my family's ranch house."

"That's because I was afraid you only wanted me to help you. I couldn't bear the thought of working for you during the day and then spending the night apart from you. I wanted to be your wife! The second time you took care of Chief, I knew I wanted you for my husband, but I feared it would always be a dream."

He cupped the side of her face. "Part of me hoped that's what was going on inside you. I had to do something fast, and told you I loved you so I wouldn't lose you. Now my heart is failing me again because you're determined to leave."

A small cry escaped her lips. "I'm not leaving if you're willing for us to face the danger together. As for the answer to the question you haven't asked me yet, it's *yes*, Roce. I want to marry the most wonderful man I've ever known. I can't imagine life without you and I'm never taking this ring off."

"So some miracles really *do* happen." He picked her up and carried her to the living room. Once he'd pulled her down on the couch with him, he proceeded to kiss them both into oblivion. "Do you know you've made me the happiest man alive?" he finally whispered against her mouth.

This was ecstasy in a new dimension. He was so carried away, it took Tracey to tell him someone was knocking on the front door. The timing was incredibly inconvenient, as usual. With a moan of protest, he eased away from her and they both walked over to the door.

A louder knock sounded. "Roce?"

"Eli?" He opened up to his brother.

"Sorry to bother you. When Wymon and I got back to the ranch house, I discovered Brianna had gone to her aunt and uncle's house. Taffy's having seizures. She begged me to come and asked me to tell you. Will you go over there to see what you can do?"

"We'll follow you."

"I'll get your doctor bag." Tracey hurried down the hall to grab it from his office.

"Sorry to leave you, Daisy. But this is one time you can't come."

He offered her a couple of doggie treats and left the house with Tracey. En route he explained about Taffy, the German shorthaired pointer who'd lived with Brianna's aunt and uncle for years. She was dying of old age.

"What can you do for her, Roce?"

"To tell you the truth, this is the kind of phone call I dread. Clark and Joanne Frost own The Saddlery in Stevensville. They're going to want to know if it's time to put their beloved dog to sleep."

"Oh…that's so hard."

"You're right. I'm afraid I've never been able to give clients that straight, heartbreaking answer they want so badly. I learned from Hannah, who listened to the owners with compassion, but always stuck to her personal opinion that it was ultimately their choice, since they knew their dog best."

"That sounds very wise."

"She was the best. For myself, I've developed a philosophy about the quality of a pet's life. Did it have more good days than bad? I've found myself in tears many times for the owners and their animals after years of emotional attachment. But no person is ready for the death of a loved one, whether a human or a pet."

"You just have to mourn with them. My horse, Spirit, is getting to that stage."

Roce reached for Tracey's hand and they drove to the Frosts' house deep in thought. He could feel the stone from the ring on her finger. Knowing it was there brought him such a fierce stab of joy, it helped mitigate the sadness he felt for the Frost family.

"One thing I do know about Taffy is that she has been deeply loved and cared for. That's what is important."

"I couldn't agree more."

When they arrived, Eli had already gone to see the dog. Brianna sat on the couch with her face awash in tears. "I'm so glad you're here, Roce. My aunt and uncle are in the study with Taffy."

"Where are the kids?"

"Libby and Stephen are with your mom."

"That's good."

"Thank heaven for her. But now that I'm here, I can't watch. I've loved Taffy too much."

Roce gave his sister-in-law a hug. "I understand, but her misery is about over."

"I hope so."

"You haven't met Tracey Marcroft yet. She's going to be my wife, but no one else knows that yet except for you and Mom."

"Oh, Roce!" she cried. "What a sad day to tell me such exciting news."

"Maybe it will help."

"I couldn't be more thrilled for you."

"While you two get acquainted, I'll see what's happening. I won't be long, sweetheart." He gave Tracey a kiss on the temple, then headed down the hall, gripping his bag.

Chapter Ten

Eli's wife smiled up at Tracey through her tears. "Come and sit down. When did you get engaged?"

Tracey checked her watch. "About an hour ago."

"Oh my gosh. That must have been right when Eli called Roce."

"He came by the house, actually."

"Have you two set a date?" the beautiful blond woman asked her.

"Not yet. I'm still trying to get used to the fact that he wants to marry me. I love him so much. You probably think we're crazy to get engaged this fast."

"Not at all. I fell in love with Eli at first sight. And you should hear Jasmine's story. She'd been seeing this other man for three months, and then they were in a plane crash, but survived. Wymon was up in the mountains and saw it happen. He rescued both of them and Jasmine fell for him on the spot."

"The Clayton brothers have a fatal charm."

"You're right." Brianna wiped her eyes. "I've learned a big secret about them. None of them are players and they don't have an agenda. But when they suddenly figure out what they want, they go after it without worrying what people will say. Nothing gets in their way."

Her comment made Tracey laugh. "That describes Roce to a T."

"Mom Clayton must be ecstatic."

"I hope so, but I haven't met her yet."

"You will, and you'll love her. How does it feel being engaged to a veterinarian?"

"I love how dedicated he is to his profession. His treatment of the injured horse at the dude ranch let me know just how exceptional he is. But I'll have to get used to being the wife of a doctor. The phone calls come at the most unexpected moments."

"I'm sure that's true. Now let me see your ring."

"I want to see yours, too. Roce told me about it."

They put out their left hands.

Tracey darted Brianna a glance. "Roce was right. Your eyes look like blue sapphires."

"And yours are an incredible violet, just like your ring. Wait till you see Jasmine's. Green as spring grass. We all have very special, unique rings."

"Those qualities define the Clayton men, too, don't you think?"

Brianna nodded with tears in her eyes. "Eli told me about the trouble at the dude ranch. I'm so sorry."

"It has been awful, but he and Wymon have been a wonderful help. I'm afraid we've put all of you in danger."

"Nonsense. The guys don't give it a thought."

"Well, *I* do. Right now we're having to take it a day at a time. I don't know what I'd do without Roce."

Tracey had just said the words when he and his brother came back into the living room.

Eli walked over and embraced his wife. "Taffy's gone. The suffering is over."

As Brianna broke down sobbing, Roce pulled Tracey close. "They asked me to put her to sleep," he whispered. "It was for the best. They have a permit to bury Taffy in the backyard, so my work is done here. Come on. Let's go home and let them grieve."

He helped her into the truck. She threw her arms around his neck. "I'm so thankful I have you, and so happy to know Daisy is there waiting for us."

"You took the words out of my mouth."

"I'm afraid I'm too happy, Roce."

He kissed her until they were both breathless. How fast everything had changed since he'd put that ring on her finger in the kitchen! Though she wanted to press herself next to him during the drive back to the house, she knew she shouldn't, and fastened her seat belt. But he grabbed her hand and clung to it all the way home.

"How did it go with Brianna?"

"She's lovely. Being able to share our engagement with her has made everything a little more real for me. We compared our rings and agreed that the Clayton men are the most extraordinary men on the planet."

Roce squeezed her hand harder. "Don't ever take off your blinders."

"I'm not wearing any. I know what I see and feel. The miracle is that you love me. When we get home, let's enjoy the picnic I fixed and curl up on the couch.

I need to hold you and start to believe I've actually found my other half."

"I want that, too, but do you mind if we save the picnic for tomorrow? This evening I want to take you out for a five-course meal and celebrate our engagement. Let's go back to the house and get dressed up."

"Oh, Roce—I'm afraid I'm still dreaming. We'll have to take some pictures on my phone and send them to both our families. Mine is going to love you so much."

"That works both ways, sweetheart. But as soon as Toly sees our announcement, he's going to be afraid to come home."

"What do you mean?"

"Three brothers down. He'll be terrified it's contagious."

She chuckled. "Every female in Montana who loves the rodeo is crazy about him. Don't tell me he doesn't have any girlfriends."

"I thought he was seeing someone, but I'm not sure if it's working out. He doesn't want to talk about it."

"Oh, well. One day I guarantee he'll wake up."

"How do you know?"

"Brianna and I have a theory about you Clayton men. You take your time, but when you suddenly figure it out, it's a done deal."

Roce's deep laughter filled the cab. It was the most wonderful sound she'd ever heard.

TRACEY COULDN'T BELIEVE it when another Saturday rolled around. Several things had been set in place during the week. They'd driven into town on Monday afternoon to pick up her car, and Roce had hired a private detective agency to keep surveillance on the house. But she hadn't heard from John yet and wondered why

Knowing they had protection reduced her fear about Wes Hunter, so she could concentrate on the love of her life. So far there'd been no incidents of any kind. She could almost believe the threat was finally over.

Not only had the days flown by and kept her busy, but she was learning more and more about Roce's profession. Every morning he was out the door to make visits to his patients on various ranches in the area.

New clients were calling or dropping by the house. Tracey realized that Roce hadn't exaggerated. He did need an assistant, and she found she loved the job. Every suffering pet that people brought in tugged on her heartstrings. Though he didn't need to check on Chief anymore, which was a relief to both of them, Tracey still felt an attachment to that horse. One day soon she hoped to see him again.

Now that the news of their engagement had gone viral and they'd celebrated at a family dinner, she and Roce were trying to decide when would be the best time to get married. They wanted it to be soon, but a lot had to be sorted out to accommodate Toly's rodeo schedule, as well as their friends and relatives both in Polson and Stevensville.

Around three on Saturday afternoon, someone rang the front doorbell. Roce should have been back by now, after going out on an emergency appointment. He didn't have another one on the books today.

Tracey hurried through the house to the front door and pressed the intercom button. "Are you here to see Dr. Clayton?"

"Yes. My name is Marcie Hewitt. He took care of my cat when he was practicing in Missoula and should have my file. Is he available?"

"He isn't here right now, but he should be back soon. Have you driven all the way from Missoula?"

"Yes."

"Then you're welcome to come in and wait. Give me a moment."

Tracey herded Daisy to the kitchen and shut the door, then hurried back through the house and unlocked the front door.

A stunning brunette dressed in a summery skirt and flouncy blouse walked inside on stylish high heels. She carried a fancy crate that held her cat.

"Please, won't you sit down?"

The other woman did as she asked. Her brown eyes played over Tracey with seeming curiosity. "I don't remember seeing you at the hospital in Missoula."

"No. My name is Tracey Marcroft. I only started working for Dr. Clayton two weeks ago."

"Are you studying to be a veterinarian?"

"No. I'm just helping out. What's wrong with your cat?"

"Sandi cries whenever she has to urinate."

"Oh, dear. The poor thing."

"When I took her to the hospital today, I found out

it was closed. There was a sign on the door with Dr. Clayton's new address. I couldn't believe he'd moved, and decided to drive straight here without making an appointment."

"You've come a long way."

"I don't trust anyone else to touch her. He's an excellent vet."

"I agree. The best. There's a bathroom down the hall if you need to freshen up."

"Thank you. I think I will."

"Do you mind if I keep your cat company?"

"Of course not, but don't open the crate."

"I won't."

She returned in a few minutes.

"Your cat is beautiful."

"She's a very expensive purebred champagne Burmese."

"You look elegant, Sandi, but I can tell you don't feel good, do you?" Tracey murmured to the animal.

She was still bent over, talking to the cat, when she heard sudden barking from the kitchen just as the front door opened. When Roce walked in, she looked up at him, but his gaze quickly went to his client.

"Marcie?"

The other woman stood up. "Well, hello, stranger. That was a fast move you made from Missoula without sending people your new address."

Tracey had the distinct impression these two knew each other beyond simply being doctor and patient. She got to her feet. "Her cat, Sandi, is in pain. If you need me, I'll be taking care of Daisy."

Without giving Roce a chance to say anything, she hurried through the house to the kitchen and got dinner started. She'd learned he was a meat-and-potatoes man, so she made stuffed pork chops and potatoes in a half shell.

Naturally, Tracey was curious about the other woman who'd shown up without an appointment, but of course an attractive man like Roce had a past. He'd probably dated several women who'd come to the surgery in Missoula. All Tracey had to remember was that he'd asked her to marry him and she had the ring on her finger to prove it.

At ten after six, he came into the kitchen and put his arms around her waist from behind. "This dinner smells fabulous."

"I hope it tastes as good." She whirled around and kissed him hard.

When he finally lifted his head, he said, "I needed that."

"Not as much as I did. You've had a long day."

"One of the sheep at the Farnon ranch has pasture bloat."

"I presume it was serious for you to be gone so long."

"I'm afraid so. I had to use a stomach tube to release the gas pressure, and then perform a rumenotomy."

"What is that?"

"It means puncturing a hole in the rumen, the first compartment of a sheep's stomach. I sutured it afterward. I'm happy to say the poor thing will recover."

"Lucky sheep."

He chuckled.

"How's the cat?" Tracey asked.

"She has a urinary tract infection. I've given her medication, but I had to draw blood and screen her for any blockages. She'll have to stay in the surgery overnight. After I check her urine again tomorrow, Marcie will be able to take her home, but I'm sure she'll be fine."

"I'm so glad. She's a beautiful-looking cat."

"I agree. The Burmese breed is exotic."

Something was going on he wasn't telling her. "Roce, dinner is ready, but since you're still busy, it'll keep."

"No, no. Come with me. We'll see Marcie out together, then we'll eat. I'm starving."

How many times had Tracey heard that? After he patted Daisy's head, they left the kitchen and walked to the doorway of the surgery.

"Marcie?" The other woman looked up from the chair placed near the cat's crate. Tracey could see Sandi was sound asleep. "When you drive back here from Missoula tomorrow, she'll be able to go home with you."

"I've decided not to go all the way back. Sandi might need me. Luckily, I was able to reserve a room for the night at the Stevensville Hotel."

Roce smiled. "The owners turned that historic place into a charming bed-and-breakfast. You'll love it."

"I'm hoping you don't have plans for tonight and will join me for dinner."

Ah. Now Tracey understood why Roce wanted her

with him. She'd love to hear the history between the two of them.

He put his arm around Tracey. "Thanks for the invitation, but I'm no longer free to accept. You met Tracey when you came in. We're engaged to be married."

Marcie got to her feet and walked over to them. Her glittering gaze centered on Tracey. "I noticed your engagement ring while you were looking at my cat. I had no idea it came from Roce."

So they *had* been on a first-name basis. "It's a sapphire from the Clayton sapphire mine. I'm still having to pinch myself." It was only the truth.

After a long pause, Marcie stared at Roce. "What time should I be by tomorrow?"

"At noon."

"I'll be here."

"If there's an emergency, I'll phone you at the hotel."

"Thank you."

"Let me see you out."

Tracey went back to the kitchen and set the table. Before long Roce came in and helped put the food out. After they sat down to eat, he reached for her hand across the table and squeezed it before letting it go.

"You'll never know my surprise when I came home. I never thought I'd see Marcie Hewitt again."

"What does she do?"

"She's an attorney."

"It's obvious you made a lasting impression on her."

"I made the mistake of eating dinner with her after I'd taken care of her cat. Hannah was still alive and asked me to give the poor girl a chance. What could it hurt? I gave in so Hannah would leave me alone. But it was a fiasco. To be honest, I'm surprised Marcie tried to go there again."

"I'm not," Tracey said. "She lives in a world of lawyers, but there's not another man out there like you and she knows it. I'm crazy about her cat."

"Sandi is cute, but it's you I'm crazy about," he said, squeezing her fingers. "Have I told you these pork chops are fantastic?"

"Dad likes them stuffed, too. I learned from watching my mom make them."

"It's time you had a treat. Tomorrow, after Marcie comes to get Sandi, we're going to take that ride in the mountains I've been promising since we met. I'll make the picnic this time and we'll go to the lake where my father used to take me and my brothers. It's so pristine you would never know man had ever been there."

"I can't wait. What about Daisy?"

"I'll phone Brianna and see if it's convenient for her to take her. I don't know if this is her weekend with Libby or not. If they have other plans, Mom will look after her."

After dinner, Tracey checked on Sandi. Later she took Daisy outside for one last time. When it was time to go to bed, Roce stayed in the office near the cat all night to make certain she didn't suffer any distress.

He was going to make the most wonderful father. Tracey didn't know if she could last until their wedding day. Once he became her husband, they would make love to each other for the rest of their lives.

THE NEXT DAY, after they'd driven up to the barn, Roce chose a spirited gelding named Moxy for Tracey to ride.

"I love my mount!"

"You're a pro and deserve the best."

"Thank you. What does Moxy stand for?"

"It's my shortened version for Chuslum Moxmox, a Nez Perce name that means 'yellow bull.' He and my horse Thunder get along great together."

"Your dark bay has Appaloosa markings. He's beautiful!"

"Jim Whitefeather, Wymon's friend who breeds Nez Perce horses, told me he's one of a kind. I've found that out. Thunder loves being in nature and knows this area of Clayton private land as well as I do."

"Is his name derived from a Nez Perce name, too?"

"Yes. It's Heinmot."

"Hmm. Heinmot and Chuslum Moxmox. Now those are names you don't hear every day."

Laughter escaped Roce's lips. No one was more fun to be with than Tracey.

They'd been climbing higher, winding through the dark green pines, when they came upon a lush meadow filled with paintbrush and lupine. This was heaven.

"Look at those delphiniums, Roce! There must be miles and miles of them interspersed with arrowroot. It makes me want to roll around in them."

Tracey's appreciation of his world made him fall deeper in love with her every day.

"Want to dismount and try it? We'll do it together."

She giggled like a young girl. "It would be our luck to squash some cute little rodent."

"As a matter of fact, there's a family of yellow-bellied marmots around here somewhere. Whenever I come up this time of year, I usually spot them."

"Ooh! I hope we see some."

"Listen hard and you might hear them whistling. They get noisy when they're disturbed."

"It's an education to be with you. You know everything."

He chuckled. "We're approaching the ridge. Watch for goats. As soon as we reach the summit, we'll drop down to a little lake."

"What's it called?"

"Hidden Lake. Not an exciting name. There must be thousands of lakes called that throughout the Rockies. Some trapper around here probably called it that when he came upon it hunting for furs. You don't know it's there until you're right on top of it."

"I bet it's beautiful."

"It is, but what you *will* find interesting is the way it's shaped, like the stunted, knobby fingers of ginger-root."

"You have to be kidding."

"I swear."

"Now I can't wait to see it."

"There's an ancient game trail that leads to the water. On any given summer night the animals come down to drink. One night we'll camp out here under the stars and watch them. It's magical."

She stared at him. "I love you, Roce."

The throb in her voice reached every atom in his body. "Better not look at me like that or I'll pull you off Moxy and we'll never make it over the ridge."

He saw her take a deep breath. "Since we don't want to hurt any of the flora or fauna around here, I'll race you there." She took off like a bullet. Before he could catch up to her, she'd reached the top in the distance.

"You're right, Chef Clayton!" she cried out in a laughing voice. "You're living up to your five-star repu-tation. It *does* look like a piece of gingerroot. That's the strangest-shaped lake I've ever seen, but it's incredibly blue and I love all the pines growing nearby."

Roce grinned and sped up. "Last person who reaches it gets tossed in."

"You're on!" Her eyes threw out a challenge and they both headed through the trees and underbrush for the water's edge. He'd never had so much fun in his life. With determination, he reached it first and jumped off Thunder.

"Come over here, baby."

"No!" she shrieked. "I didn't bring extra clothes."

"That's all right. You can wrap up in Moxy's blan-ket. If all else fails, you've got me to keep you warm."

She shook her head. "You wouldn't!"

"I'm afraid I would." He reached her in a few swift strides and pulled her off her horse.

"Roce! No!"

"No, what? Let's see what a good swimmer you are."

He carried her over to the shore where the under-growth wasn't quite as dense. She wrapped her arms around his neck, clinging to him for dear life. "If you throw me in, you go in with me, Roce Clayton."

"What will you do for me if I grant you a reprieve?" They were both breathing hard.

"Anything!"

"Marry me a week from tomorrow. I refuse to wait until July 29. That's five weeks away. It might as well be a hundred."

"But our families—we've already settled on that date."

"I've changed my mind."

"Then Toly won't be able to come. We can't do this to everyone." Tracey kissed Roce's chin.

"Yes, we can. It's *our* wedding."

She bit her lip. "But if half of them can't be here—"

"That's too bad."

"You don't really mean that. Roce, be reasonable."

"What if I don't want to be?" He felt out of control, and holding her this close wasn't helping.

"I think we're having our first fight." Her anxious eyes coaxed him to give up. "Maybe if you eat. Please put me down and we'll set out the food you made."

"Food isn't going to fix what's wrong."

In the next second he felt something zing over his right shoulder, missing it by a couple inches. Roce lowered Tracy into the shrubs and covered her with his body.

"Someone is shooting at us. Don't move."

He pulled out his phone and sent a group text to his brothers and Luis.

Sniper on the loose at Hidden Lake. Almost got shot.
Don't know if he's working alone. Bring help quick.

Tracey clutched at his arms. Her body was shak-
ing. "Who'd be shooting at us? Wes has problems, but
he's not a killer."

"I agree. Whoever took that shot hasn't tried it
again. Maybe it's one of his friends trying to give us a
scare, since you weren't spooked away from the area
by the slashed tires."

"But how do any of them know where we are when
the surveillance team is guarding the house?"

"I'm sure one of the cohorts has been keeping tabs
on us from a distance and phones Wes to keep him ap-
prised. Let's hope he thinks that warning shot has put
the fear in us."

"It has," Tracey admitted.

Roce kissed her forehead. "I know. I'm heavy. Forgive me."

"Do you think I'm even noticing?"

She was a wonder. "Lie still while I whistle for
Thunder," he replied.

Over the last few years he'd played games with his
horse and had trained him to come on his signal, But
Roce had never imagined having to rely on him to follow through in a life-or-death situation. Two low whis-
tles and his horse's ears twitched before he walked over
to the bushes where they were hiding. Moxy followed.

"Don't move, my love."

"I promise."

Stealthily, Roce got to his feet and reached for his

rifle. "Good boy, Thunder." While his horse stood there, he removed the saddlebag. After resting his body against the trunk of a pine tree, he opened the bag and got out an apple.

"What are you doing?"

He knew the direction the bullet had come from—a little ways above the lake and farther along the shore. "I'm going to throw this apple into the water and draw the sniper's fire, if he's still around."

"Be careful, Roce." Fear laced Tracey's voice.

"Always."

Positioning himself on the other side of the tree, he threw the apple the same way he used to skip rocks with his brothers, making as much noise as possible. Sure enough, he heard more gunfire, but the sniper was way off the mark.

Roce lifted his own rifle and looked through the scope. When he saw movement, he shot three times, then waited for return fire. There was none, but he could hear the sound of rotors in the distance.

"That's a helicopter," Tracey whispered.

"Thank God."

"Can I sit up now?"

He pulled her to her feet and sheltered her in his arms while they watched two forest service choppers circle the area where the first shot had come from. A minute later his phone rang. Wymon's caller ID. Roce clicked on and put it on speaker so Tracey could hear.

"Wymon?"

"You're a crack shot, Roce. You got Grady Cox in the leg."

"Grady was the shooter?" Tracey's voice shook.

"He was trying to reach a forest service truck he'd stolen and left up here near the top of the ridge. The thug is dressed in a forest service uniform."

"*That's* how he got access to the property without being suspected," Roce murmured. "The surveillance crew wouldn't have noticed anything out of the ordinary. These mountains are laced with roads, to give better access in case of fire."

"Be assured Cox isn't going anywhere now except to jail. We have more breaking news. Wes Hunter took off from his job at the fruit farm today. No one saw him leave. To make things worse, Mr. Farnon, the owner, discovered one of his rifles was missing."

"Oh, no." Tracey burrowed her face against Roce's chest.

"Wes is still on the loose and we were just informed that Ramon Cruz is also missing from his father's ranch."

"That doesn't surprise me." Roce kissed his shivering fiancée.

"Are you two all right?"

Roce looked into Tracey's eyes. Though shaken, she nodded. "We will be," he said. "You guys got here in record time."

"There's a reason for that. When Farnon called Sheldon about Wes's disappearance, he also notified the sheriff, and a manhunt was already under way to look for him."

"How did you find out?"

"John called me and Eli to let us know what was

going on and to warn us that Wes is armed. We checked with your surveillance crew, but they hadn't seen anyone come around your house. When they checked their video tapes, though, they spotted a forest service truck that had been driving by the house all week."

"Incredible. Right under our noses."

"The instant Eli and I got your text, we assumed it was Wes and came in the second helicopter."

"That's two down out of the gang of four."

"Now it's down to Cruz, working behind the scenes with Wes like an evil tag team," Eli said, breaking in.

"Hey, bro."

"With the help of the police we're going to track down these goons. It won't be long before we close in on them. In case they're hiding out up here, we've asked the pilot to hover over you until you reach the ranch house safely."

Roce was so thankful for his brothers he could hardly talk, given the boulder-sized lump that had suddenly lodged in his throat. "Have I ever told you guys you're the best?"

"We feel the same way about you. Wymon and I have been talking. The two of you should stay at the ranch house until this is over."

"Agreed," Roce said. "I don't want clients coming to the surgery to be targets or to be taken hostage by those two. I'll have to give advice over the phone or ask patients to seek out another vet while the hospital is closed."

"We'll pick up Daisy and bring her to you. Later you can go back for the things you need."

Roce hung up and hugged Tracey once more. She clung to him. "Look what has happened since I came to the dude ranch. Because of me, you've gotten involved and could have been killed just now." She broke down sobbing.

"Hush, sweetheart." He covered her tearstained face with kisses. "No one could have known something like this would happen."

"But it would have been my fault. To think your life might have been snuffed out. I can't stand it."

"I honestly don't believe Wes or his friends intended to kill anyone, but they do have serious issues. Grady and Simmonds need therapy, and hopefully they'll get it once their families are notified."

"How can you be so calm about this?"

"Because I've got my warrior fiancée with me." Thank God she was alive and safe in his arms. This close call reminded him how precious life was. Hers was the most precious of all.

He heard her give a little laugh. "Don't be silly."

Encouraged, he said, "Do you think you can handle the ride back? Otherwise we'll drive home in the forest service truck."

"I feel perfectly safe with you and the horses." After giving him a passionate kiss he would remember for the rest of his life, she wiped the tears from her face and mounted Moxy before he could help her. Another woman might have fallen apart, but not this angel who'd transformed his life.

Roce threw the saddlebag back on Thunder and

mounted him, keeping hold of his rifle in case he needed it again. "Come on, sweetheart. Let's go home."

She rode by his side. With the helicopter flying overhead, the pilot keeping watch for Wes and Ramon, Roce knew she'd let go of her fear enough to handle it. They made quick time retracing their path down the mountain. A welcoming committee consisting of Solana, his mother and Luis, who'd assembled some ranch hands, was waiting for them at the barn. He handed Luis his rifle to take care of.

Roce's mom kissed both of them and ushered them into the house, while a couple hands took care of the horses. "A guest room is ready for you, Tracey. Solana will take you upstairs so you can freshen up."

Roce turned to his wife-to-be. "While you do that, I'll run to the house and bring the things we'll need to get us through until tomorrow."

"That's a good idea," his mom said. "Dinner is almost ready. After you get back, we'll eat and talk."

"Sounds good. I'll hurry," he whispered against Tracey's ear.

"Be careful. If I lost you now…"

"No one's losing anybody."

He took off. Within two minutes he reached his house, ahead of his brothers. The surveillance crew acknowledged him before he pulled out the remote to get inside. Daisy gave him one of her heartwarming welcomes.

After he took her outside and refreshed her water, he went to the office to check his messages. One was important. He'd take care of it when he got back to his mom's.

Roce had never gone in the bedroom Tracey was sleeping in, but she'd need a few items to get her through until tomorrow. He pulled a suitcase from his upstairs closet and threw in the items he'd need. Then he went back down to pack what he hoped would be enough for her.

Her periwinkle-blue sweater caught his eye and he put it on top of her other clothes. While he was in the bathroom gathering her toiletries, his phone rang. It was Eli.

"We're back and saw your truck out in front. You got home fast. Do you need any help?"

"I'm fine. All I have to do is load Daisy. Thanks more than you know for what you did today."

"We're thanking the powers-that-be that neither you or Tracey were shot up there, or worse."

"Amen to that. I'll see you at the ranch house in a few minutes. Mom has dinner waiting for us." Before he hung up he said, "Eli?"

"What is it?"

Roce would never forget the way their father had been accidentally shot and killed by a hunter. None of them would. "You and Wymon need to be extra careful. You're a target now, too."

"We hear you," his brother said. His voice told Roce that they were on the same wavelength.

"Good." He hung up and walked to the front door with the suitcase. "Come on, Daisy. We're going for a little ride."

She knew those words well enough and fought to get out the door first, producing his first smile since the shooting.

Chapter Eleven

Monday morning, Tracey came down to the dining room, and Solana brought her breakfast. Halfway through the delicious meal of pancakes and sausage, Roce walked in, clean-shaven and dressed in a Western shirt and jeans. Daisy followed at his heels.

Tracey was learning his moods and recognized that he was in a hurry. He came around the table and kissed her, just as Solana appeared. "Ready to eat?"

He lifted his head. "Thanks, but I've got to go help a mare having trouble giving birth."

"I guess that's more important," Tracey murmured. Of course it was. She wanted to go with him, but he hadn't asked her to. That was because he wanted her home and safe. "At least have one of my sausage links." She held one up to his mouth and he ate it on the spot.

"Thanks for sharing."

"I'll miss you. Hurry back."

"I shouldn't be too long. A normal delivery only takes fifteen to twenty minutes and the Ellis ranch is nearby. I've been on the phone with Mrs. Ellis, a new client. I went out there last week to check on their pregnant Thoroughbred. Her husband is in Great Falls on business and their regular vet is away on vacation, so I got the call."

"At the rate you're attracting business, you'll soon be turning clients away." Tracey jumped up from the table. "I'll walk you out to the truck. Have you got your bag?"

"Right here." He'd left it at the front door.

Together they walked outside under a hot sun. Living at the large ranch house, a masterpiece of Western architecture and history, was so different from living at his house. Though Tracey was treated like a queen here, she ached for them to be back in their own little piece of heaven.

"Promise me you'll stay safe."

"You're the one I worry about." He cradled her face in his hands. They kissed long and hard for a few moments. But she could tell he was anxious to leave, and relinquished his mouth first.

"I love you, Roce Clayton. Drive safely."

After he drove away, she took Daisy for a short walk, then went upstairs with her, where Tracey phoned her family. She told them the details of yesterday's close call in the mountains, playing it down and assuring them she was perfectly safe. Before long the police would catch Wes Hunter and his friend. Then she and Roce could concentrate on the upcoming wedding.

In her heart she didn't want to wait five more weeks any more than Roce did, but they couldn't change the date now. She talked to her mom awhile longer. When the threat of danger was completely over, they would shop for a wedding dress in Missoula. Roce believed the men would be caught any day now. Tracey was hanging on to that hope.

She looked down at Daisy, who needed to go outside again. They went back downstairs. When they came in, she saw Roce's mother in the hallway. Because of the danger, she hadn't gone to the gem shop up on the mountain yet.

"It's after one. Are you hungry for lunch, Tracey?"

"Well, I've been waiting for Roce to get back so we could eat together."

His mother frowned. "He's been gone a long time." Tracey thought so, too. "I guess the mare had complications."

Both women were worried, with good reason. "I'll try to reach him." Tracey pulled out her phone and called him. There was no answer and it went to his voice mail. She asked him to phone her and let her know when he'd be home.

"Something must have come up. He'll call when he can."

"Then let's go in the dining room and eat."

Over sandwiches and salad, they talked about wedding plans, but when it got to be three o'clock, neither of them could hide their concern. Roce's mom called Wymon and told him why she was worried.

He'd been up at the pasture with Eli, but upon hearing the news, they both came home. The second they walked in, Tracey met them at the door. "I have this feeling something is wrong. Will you drive me to the Ellis ranch?"

"We'll go," Eli told her. "You stay here with Mom."

"No." She shook her head. "If he's in trouble, he'll need all our help."

"Good," Mrs. Clayton declared. "While you're gone, I'm phoning the sheriff to tell him our concerns. If it's nothing, I don't care."

"All right," Eli said. "Let's go."

Tracey gave Roce's mom a hug before hurrying outside. Wymon helped her into the front seat of Eli's truck and got in the back. Eli climbed behind the wheel and sped down the hill to the highway.

"When we get there, you need to stay in the truck, Tracey. Don't argue with us on this. We'll get out first and check if everything is all right."

"Okay."

They reached the small ranch in a few minutes. Tracey's heart kicked against her ribs when she spotted Roce's truck parked outside the barn. She didn't see another vehicle. Her first instinct was to race inside, but she knew she had to let his brothers take charge.

Wymon squeezed her hand. "Keep your head down."

She nodded and stretched out across the seat so she could still see through the other window. The two brothers entered the barn. Within five minutes they came back out. Eli raced to the ranch house, while Wymon hurried to the truck.

His face was dark. "Someone shot and killed the mare. Roce isn't here."

A pained cry escaped from Tracey's lips. "That explains why his truck is still here. He's been kidnapped. I just know it." Tears gushed down her face. "Wes has had eyes everywhere. He must have ambushed Roce after he arrived at the Ellis ranch to deliver the foal. Wes could have taken him anywhere."

"We'll find him, Tracey." Wymon got on the phone to the sheriff to report what had happened, and learned the police were on their way. In the next minute Eli came running to the truck.

"When I asked Mrs. Ellis to describe the man who came on the property, she said he was Hispanic."

Tracey gasped. "I bet it was Ramon Cruz. That means he and Wes have taken Roce."

"He locked Mrs. Ellis in the basement so she couldn't get out. She's really shaken up, but she wasn't hurt. We've called her husband to come home. Her married daughter is on her way over. I made her some coffee and left her lying on the couch until the police get here."

No sooner had Eli spoken than three patrol cars pulled in. The next fifteen minutes passed in a blur while the sheriff talked to all of them and got the details from Mrs. Ellis.

All the time they were talking, Tracey could hardly breathe for the pain. She couldn't comprehend Ramon Cruz's motive for doing any of it, including shooting the pregnant mare.

"We've got to find Roce!"

Everyone turned to her. Wymon put his arm around her shoulders and helped her to the truck. "The police have put out a statewide search. Dr. Cruz is doing everything he can to cooperate. While the police are scouring this part of Montana, I'm going to drive us back to the ranch house. Eli will follow in Roce's truck."

Wymon started the engine and they took off for the Clayton ranch. She stared at him. "Where do you think they could have taken him?"

"I wish I knew, Tracey."

"Well, I'm going to call John. He and Sheldon have to have some inkling of where Wes would have gone." She reached in her pocket for her phone, but the call went to John's voice mail and she clicked off.

"Wymon? Will you drive me to the dude ranch? Everything started there. I don't know why, but I have a feeling we'll get answers if we talk to John and Sheldon."

"I trust your instincts." He got on his phone to tell his wife what was going on. Then he called his mother. Lastly he and Eli had a long conversation. When he clicked off, he put a comforting hand on Tracey's arm. "Eli's right behind us. We'll do whatever it takes to find Roce, Tracey."

"I know you will." She struggled not to break down, but wasn't successful. "I can't lose Roce. He's my whole life. To go through this again will be the end of me."

"What do you mean?"

"Over a year and a half ago, the man I'd planned to marry was killed while deployed overseas. I thought I was going to die. When I met Roce, I realized my life wasn't over. He made me happy to be alive again. I love him with all my heart and soul. This just couldn't happen again. There's no one like Roce. Daisy would go into permanent mourning, like me."

"I'm sure he's alive, Tracey. You have to believe that."

She wiped her eyes with both hands, but the tears kept coming. "I do. I'll keep believing it until I can't."

During the twenty-minute drive she listened as Wymon talked on and off with family and with his police friend who worked at the criminal database. Before they turned off for the dude ranch, Toly called him and they talked the rest of the way.

Wymon drove up to the ranch house. The second he parked, Tracey jumped out and ran inside to find John. The new guests had gone into the dining room for dinner, and she raced past Colette, who was running the front desk. Wymon followed her to John's office, where she found John, along with Sylvia, Sheldon and their other sons, Paul and Thad.

The moment John saw her he welcomed them inside. "You poor dear." He got up from the desk and hugged her. "You'll never know how devastated we are that Wes and his friends have done these terrible things to you. I'm glad you and Roce's brothers are here. We've been planning a strategy. I promise we'll find him."

Tracey couldn't ask for more than that.

Sylvia eyed her with a solemn expression. "Sit down, honey, We can't comprehend that Wes and his friends have taken things this far and brought us to this impasse."

Tracey leaned forward. "Does his therapist have any idea where he might have taken Roce? Any idea at all?"

Sheldon spoke up. "No. I've talked to him. It's a long story. My son's flawed view of his world was developed in childhood, when he couldn't have everything he wanted. His sense of entitlement, combined with his sense of deprivation, has caused him to blame me and my father whenever anything goes wrong. He doesn't own up to responsibility.

"I'm afraid he has delusions of becoming a very wealthy man and doesn't care how he achieves it. He grew up around horses and knows their value. In time he hoped to steal enough horses from the ones I've been buying for dad. He thought to sell them in return for a nest egg that would set him up.

"I've tried to reason with him. With hard work he could achieve his goal, but he refuses to listen and has been taking shortcuts that have landed him in serious trouble. You and Dr. Clayton got in his way when you noticed Chief's limp. That started this latest crisis."

Tracey took a deep breath. "He's been focused on the two of us for the last three weeks. That fixation has never gone away, even after I left the dude ranch." She got to her feet. "The one thing that bothered me the most about him was the way he acted as if he owned the stable, like it was his private property. I fear he's going to hurt Roce for invading his space."

She stared at Sheldon. "I'm sure the police have asked you this, but is there a place on the dude ranch where he likes to go when he wants to get away from everyone?"

"Not that I'm aware of. Normally he goes off to Darby with his friends."

"Or you *think* that's where he's gone," Wymon interjected. "But what if he's holding our brother somewhere on this property that's particularly familiar to him."

Tracey stared at Roce's brother. "That's it! I think I know where that is. Rocky Point. It's the perfect place to hide out."

Sheldon nodded. "You've reminded me. He sometimes camped out up there in the off season with his friends."

She got excited. "There's one of those old dilapidated survival huts still left from a hundred and fifty years ago when they ran sheep. I remember pointing it out to the children on one of our rides.

"We got off the horses and started climbing around the boulders to reach it. But Wes wouldn't allow it. He told us to get back on the horses because it was too dangerous. I couldn't understand it."

John nodded. "I remember you telling me that."

Eli and Wymon exchanged glances. "That could be his hideout. He and Ramon could have taken Roce on one of the back roads to reach it, and are holding him there, where no one would think to find him. Let's go."

"I'm coming with you," Tracey stated.

His brothers eyed her and nodded.

"I'll lead the way," Sheldon declared. "You can follow me. I know exactly which road to take. There'll be enough moonlight that we shouldn't need to use our headlights. If my son has done this to Dr. Clayton, then he's going to have to deal with me."

John eyed Tracey through watery eyes. "He *has* to be found! I'm calling the sheriff now. He'll coordinate a thorough search with you and the forest service. They'll bring in the helicopters."

Tracey ran out to Wymon's truck and jumped in.

While they were on their way she prayed over and over again. *Please, God. Let Roce be alive. Just let him be alive.*

ROCE FELT AS IF he was the victim of bad guys in an old Louis L'Amour western. They'd tied his arms behind his back and bound his ankles. With a scarf blinding his eyes, he couldn't see a thing, and he'd been dumped on the ground like a sack of potatoes. Wherever he'd been brought, he'd probably been there eight hours. It was getting cold.

Mrs. Ellis had told him she'd meet him in the barn, but when he'd arrived, Ramon was waiting for him with a gun and had tied him up. "Grady was supposed to finish you off. Since he didn't, I'll have to do the honors."

Except it hadn't happened yet. Roce guessed it would be over when Wes made the call. He wouldn't have thought they'd actually want to kill him.

The memory of Ramon shooting the suffering mare would have haunted him forever if he hadn't known she wouldn't live through the delivery of twins, a rare occurrence. It was the last sight he saw before he was blindfolded and dragged into the trunk of a car, probably belonging to Mrs. Ellis.

He had no idea where he'd been taken, but judging by the strong smell of pines and the sounds of forest life, it was in the mountains. After all he and Tracey had been through, he knew she had to be in agony. By now everyone he loved would be out looking for him.

You didn't have to drown for your life to flash before your eyes. But the review playing in his head kept getting interrupted by the fight that had broken out between his two kidnappers. The amount of alcohol they'd been consuming didn't help. He could smell it when they walked over to check on him. Each time they approached, one of them kicked him.

"What are you waiting for, Wes?"

"I want him to know what it feels like for your life to be over. I want him to suffer for interfering. I could have made a ton of money off Chief. The perfect Dr. Clayton has millions in the bank and everything else he ever wanted. Horses. A ranch. A snooty hot babe who thinks she's Miss Rodeo of America. They both have my grandfather whipped. It isn't fair, Ramon."

"You're talking crazy. Come on. Let's off him and leave the state. I switched out the license plates on that old woman's car. We can be hundreds of miles away from here by tomorrow. His body won't be found for years. It's the perfect plan."

"I want to watch him squirm some more."

"You're not thinking straight. Do whatever you want. I'm leaving."

"The hell you are!"

"Then kill him now! Here's the gun."

In the silence that followed, Roce knew his life was about to end. Tracey's name was in his heart and on his lips when he heard other voices.

A gun went off. Suddenly someone was kneeling by him, someone with the flowery scent he associated with the woman he loved.

He was incredulous. "Tracey?"

"Yes, my darling. We found you in time, thank God." She removed the scarf so he could see her beautiful face. It was covered in tears. In the distance he saw clusters of headlights and heard shouting.

"I'll have you untied in a minute. Your arms must be aching." He could hear her low sobs. "There."

Released at last, he rolled over and sat up, flexing his stiff, cramped shoulders. His wrists had rope burns, but at the moment he hardly felt them as he shakily drew her into his arms and rocked her, unable to believe this was happening. "I was afraid I'd never see you again." Tears oozed from his own eyes. "I never prayed so hard in my life. And now you're here."

"I came up with Eli and Wymon." She eased away from him long enough to start undoing the ropes binding his ankles. It took a few minutes, but she finally freed them.

Roce rubbed them before slowly getting to his feet with Tracey's help. "Where did they bring me?"

"Rocky Point."

He moaned. "So close to home. How did you know?"

"Sheldon was trying to help us when I asked if Wes had a favorite area on the dude ranch where he liked to hang out. That's when I thought about the trail ride that day when Wes told us to get back on the horses."

"So I owe my life to *you*." Roce was in danger of kissing the life out of her.

"It was all of us working together. Eli found Mrs. Ellis unharmed, but locked in her basement. She described the man who entered her house with a gun. It was Ramon. He stole her car. She said he was drunk."

"That's true. I could smell his breath. He dragged me into the trunk after killing the pregnant mare. She was carrying twins. All three of them needed help and would have died, anyway."

"How awful for you."

"When a man is under the influence, he's capable of doing a lot of things. Wes and Ramon should never have a drop of alcohol again. I still don't think they're killers, but they'll need to be put in a serious rehab program for a long time."

"When we knew you'd been kidnapped, we alerted the police and drove to the dude ranch to meet with John and his family. Everyone contributed, and now it's all over. Really over."

"It is, bro," another person said.

His brothers came over and hugged him hard.

"As I've told you many times, you guys are the best."

Eli smiled. "That works both ways. Do you know you don't look that bad for someone who has been to hell and back?" They all laughed.

"The gun was shot out of Ramon's hand, but no one was killed here tonight," Wymon explained. "The sheriff has taken both of them into custody. They've been arrested and will be booked in jail before being taken before the judge. Our part here is done."

Tracey hugged Roce harder.

"The sheriff will get statements from you tomorrow. Come get in the truck," Eli urged. "We'll drive you two back to the ranch, where your truck is parked."

"I'll drive us home from there." Tracey covered Roce's face with kisses.

He kissed her back. "Do you have any idea how good that sounds?"

An hour later, after phone calls to both sets of parents and Toly, letting them know all was well, they reached his house and went inside. Tracey walked Roce down the hall to the staircase. "Go on up and shower while I fix you whatever you want."

"Breakfast."

"Breakfast it is."

He stood under the shower, savoring the soap and hot water. After toweling himself off, he threw on a robe. While he sat on the side of his king-size bed to rub some ointment into the rope burns on his wrists and ankles, Tracey entered his bedroom. It was the first time she'd ever been up there.

She'd laden the tray with crisp bacon, crepes, orange juice and coffee. All his favorites. Without saying anything, he took it from her and put it on the end of the bed. Then he pulled her into his arms.

"Before I need food, I need you."

Their mouths met in a feverish conflagration. The desire to become one with her was fast taking over. "I can't believe how close I came to never knowing this joy again."

"Don't think about it. I'm not going to. Our whole life is ahead of us, with no shadows. But Eli said it best—you've been to hell and back. I know you're hurting *and* ravenous. Come on. Let's eat before the food gets cold."

She eased out of his arms and moved the tray to the middle of the bed before stretching out on one side of it. He took the hint. But when he propped himself to face her, he felt a pain in his ribs where one of the guys' boots had connected.

"I heard that moan," she said, and handed him a small bottle of painkillers. "Tomorrow we'll visit the clinic in Stevensville and get an X-ray."

"I'm the doctor around here and don't need that kind of help."

"But I'm your wife-to-be. Please do it for me."

"How can I say no to that?" He took four pills immediately with his juice. Then he dug in. They were both starving and ate everything.

"Do you want more?"

Roce removed the tray and put it on the floor. After turning off the lamp, he got back on the bed and rolled her toward him. "I just want to hold you for a little while and count my blessings."

TRACEY WOKE UP late the next morning, still dressed in the clothes she'd gone to bed in. She turned her head on the pillow. Roce was still sound asleep. Last night she'd planned to leave the room the moment he'd started kissing her, but at some point they'd both fallen asleep. After the nightmare he'd lived through, he would probably sleep half the day.

She slid off the bed and took the tray downstairs. The knowledge that all the bad actors were now in jail made her giddy. Tracey took a shower and washed her hair. She picked out a pair of jeans and a Western blouse to put on. Once she'd pulled on her cowboy boots, she wrote a note that she'd gone over to his mother's, and left it on the kitchen counter.

A partly cloudy sky greeted her as she hurried out of the house to her car. They needed their things back, especially Roce's razor.

"Alberta…" She hugged Roce's mother the second she opened the door, and they both shed tears of relief. But somehow Daisy got between them, causing them to laugh.

Tracey kissed the dog's silky head. "I've missed you, too, and there's someone else who can't wait to see you. Come on and help me gather our stuff."

It didn't take long to carry everything out to her car. Daisy ran circles around her and jumped in the front seat of the vehicle.

"Look at that," Alberta exclaimed. "Just like a person."

"Daisy thinks she is." The two women laughed again.

"Don't be strangers."

"Are you kidding? Your boys worship you, and so do I. You've raised the most incredible son in creation."

"If I did any good, he's proved it by choosing the loveliest woman in the world to marry. All my boys can't say enough about you."

"If they hadn't known what to do, we wouldn't have figured things out in time. I promise we'll see you very soon."

Excitement swept through Tracey as she drove to the house, knowing Roce was there and safe. She made two trips inside. On the first one, Daisy dashed up the stairs. When Tracey came in the second time, she could hear Roce's deep laughter. Someone was awake. The sound thrilled her heart.

She took his things up to his room so he could use his toiletries. Daisy had gotten up on the bed and was enjoying a good rub behind the ears.

"Well, aren't you two the happiest pair I've ever seen?"

"I feel like a new man. All I need is a kiss from you."

"I can do that."

When she walked over to the bed, he pulled her down, but then moaned again.

"Uh-oh. It sounds like you have a bruised rib." She kissed him briefly and stood up. "You've got to be more careful. I'm going downstairs to fix your breakfast. What sounds good?"

"Anything."

"Okay. Come on, Daisy. You need your food, too."

The mention of food did the trick. The dog followed her down and waited while she filled her bowls. With that done, Tracey got busy fixing Roce some French toast and ham.

"Roce?" she called to him. "Breakfast is ready."

"Coming." He walked into the kitchen looking drop-dead gorgeous in a silky burgundy shirt and tan pants.

"Wow." It was all she could manage to say.

"That word describes my feelings every time I see you. Just don't squeeze me too hard." He put his arms around her neck and gave her a kiss that made her forget everything else.

"I don't think I can restrain myself. Maybe we'd better sit down and eat."

She poured coffee while he did her bidding.

"Life doesn't get better than this," she said as they tucked into the meal.

His eyes narrowed on her mouth. "Oh, yes it does. What do you say we get on a plane right now and fly to Reno to get married?"

"I haven't stopped thinking about it since you almost threw me in the lake."

"A funny thing happened to me before I could do that. It gave me time to rethink what it was I wanted."

Tears made her eyes smart. She reached across the table to grasp his hand. "Our families are too wonderful for us to do something that won't include all of them."

He nodded.

On cue, the doorbell sounded. They both smiled in resignation. "I'll get it." Roce got up from the table. She and Daisy followed him into the living room.

"Sheriff Garson—come in."

"I'm very relieved to see you up and uninjured, considering what you were put through, Dr. Clayton. All I need is a statement from you two and I'll leave you alone."

"Would you like coffee?" Tracey offered.

"I'd like it very much if you don't mind."

"I've got some hot. Do you want cream? Sugar?"

"Just black."

Tracey poured him a mug and brought it in. They sat around the coffee table and answered his questions.

"I feel so sorry for the parents of these men," Tracey said. "John and Sheldon tried so hard to give Wes a second chance."

The sheriff nodded. "So did Dr. Cruz. We're still trying to reach the parents of Simmons and Cox. Simmonds has been charged with breaking and entering and vehicular theft. Cox faces charges of assault with a deadly weapon and will be going to prison."

Tracey groaned at the litany of charges.

"Ramon Cruz has been charged with drunkenness, kidnapping and aggravated assault with a deadly weapon on Dr. Clayton, Mrs. Ellis and on the pregnant mare, resulting in the death of three animals.

"Wes Hunter will face prison time for drunkenness, criminal contempt of court, kidnapping and assault and battery. It's a very sad thing that four men, still in their twenties, have already ruined their lives. The good news today is that they didn't ruin yours."

Tracey leaned forward. "I can't thank you enough for being there and helping us. And please, will you thank the forest service pilots for their help at Hidden Lake? Everyone played a part."

"I certainly will." He got to his feet. "Hopefully, when we see each other again, it'll be for entirely different reasons."

"Amen to that." Roce walked him out.

Tracey went back to the kitchen. While she was loading the dishwasher, her cell phone rang. It was her family. They all got on the line while she told them the details of their harrowing experience. Roce came in during the conversation and added his thoughts.

"Your daughter knew where I'd been taken. She was the one who found me. I owe her my life. Our wedding day can't come soon enough."

They spoke awhile longer before she hung up. Roce had already finished the dishes. She turned to him. "What can I do for you?"

"I need to check my messages and call a couple of patients. Then let's give some thought to a honeymoon."

"Can you take off that kind of time while you're building your practice here?"

He put his arm around her shoulders and they walked down the hall to his office. "You only get one honeymoon. My practice will survive. I'll ask Dr. Cruz to cover for me. Maybe extending my friendship will help us all to heal."

"For you to do that makes you the most remarkable person I've ever known."

"He'll probably turn me down, but it wouldn't hurt to ask."

"I agree. Now tell me something. Where do you want to go after the reception?"

"I was hoping you'd tell me."

"Really? How about flying to the Greek islands and chartering a boat so we can go wherever we want?"

"While I'm on the phone, why don't you look up some websites and see what we can arrange."

She shook her head. "Roce—I was only teasing."

His expression grew serious. "No, you weren't. As far as I'm concerned it sounds perfect."

"You're just saying that because you always put me first. I want you to be honest with me."

He started to laugh and gripped her shoulders. "Are we having our second fight?"

Put that way, she felt silly, and laughed, too. "I love you so much, and I'm going crazy waiting for our wedding day."

"You mean you don't feel married yet, living with me?"

"No, because it's not official."

"That's not the only reason, sweetheart." Heat filled her cheeks. "But there's one thing we need to do and can do today. If you'll get ready, we'll swing by the county courthouse to get our marriage license."

Chapter Twelve

July 28

"Roce? I Hate to bother you the day before your wedding, but this is an emergency only you will want to deal with."

His stomach clenched. Since the kidnapping he'd known nothing but happiness. "What's wrong, Luis?"

"It's about Thunder. Come to the barn."

Roce groaned. "I'll be right there."

He shot up from the chair in his office where he'd been working, and hurried through the house to the kitchen with his doctor bag. "Sorry, Daisy. Got to go. Tracey went to town to do some last-minute errands, but she'll be back soon." He gave her a treat before heading out the front door.

If Thunder was in real trouble, he'd have no choice but to call on Dr. Cruz's help sooner than he'd imagined. He and the broken-hearted older vet had talked often since the arrest of his son, and had become friends. Arrangements had already been made for him to care for a couple of Roce's patients while he was in Greece with Tracey.

Their agreement was reciprocal. When he needed to visit Ramon at the Montana State Prison, Roce would cover for him.

But knowing that something serious was wrong with his horse was like getting stomped on by a bull. Thunder was more human than animal. Roce would never forget that day at Hidden Lake. Because of his horse's intelligence, he'd been able to reach his rifle and fight off their sniper before he or Tracey had been shot.

He drove through the ranch entrance and up the road to the barn at full speed. Toly would be flying in later today. Roce had planned to drive to the Missoula airport with his brothers to pick him up, but he'd probably have to give that a miss.

By the time he reached the barn, he wasn't in the best shape. Slamming on his brakes, he leaped from the cab and hurried inside to Thunder's stall. Luis was standing at the opening, as if he didn't want him to see what was wrong.

Roce swallowed hard. "How bad is it?"

Luis had never looked so anxious, filling Roce with dread. "Eli's waiting for you in the tack room. I think you should talk to him first."

He sucked in his breath before racing toward it. When he flew inside, the door shut behind him and he heard his brothers yell, "Surprise!"

For the first time in his life he came close to fainting. They'd just pulled off his bachelor party! So that was why Tracey had suddenly decided she needed to drive in to Stevensville.

When he realized there was nothing wrong with his horse and that all was well in his world, he wheeled around. Toly's was the first face he saw. His brother had flown in early.

"Toly—you're a sight for sore eyes." They hugged hard.

"Glad to see you, bro."

Two more powerful hugs from his brothers followed. It was a good thing his bruised ribs had healed or he'd be headed for the hospital.

Eli passed a sack of doughnuts around. They'd put sodas on the table in the corner. Wymon handed him an eight-by-ten-inch brown envelope. "We wished we could have done this in style tonight, but there's not enough time. What we did do was get together with Mom and this is what we came up with."

Roce downed two doughnuts before opening the envelope. He found two items inside. One was a plan of the Clayton property. A big circle had been drawn in red around the lower left half. The other item was a deed, made out to him.

He lifted his head in confusion. "What's this?"

"Your portion of Clayton land. It's all yours. You can build a big house for all the children you and Tracey are going to have, erect a state-of-the-art kennel for your surgery, construct your own barn for your horses, and anything else you want. Mom said this was Dad's dream for you after you stopped competing in the rodeo."

Roce remembered that painful period as if it were yesterday. He remembered his father's kindness and wisdom. His belief in Roce had been the turning point in his life. He was too choked up to think, let alone talk.

"You okay?" Toly asked.

"I don't know what to say. You guys are the best."

"We know," Eli quipped.

They all laughed.

By now Luis had come inside, wearing a grin. "Don't kill me, Roce. I had to come up with an excuse you couldn't turn down."

"Well, you sure did know how to do that!" Roce gave the foreman a huge hug. He and Solana might not be blood, but they were part of the family.

He stared at Wymon. "Was Tracey in on this?"

"Yes, but she doesn't know about the gift. That's for you to tell her."

"Yeah." Eli smiled. "One night below a Greek moon, while you're walking through white sand."

"You lucky devil," Toly murmured.

Roce nodded. "I know."

July 29

LITTLE LIBBY LOOKED adorable in a long, white lace dress with a purple sash. As soon as the organ music started, she walked down the aisle of the church in Polson, holding a bouquet of larkspurs.

Behind her came Roce's two sisters-in-law and Tracey's best friend dressed in soft lavender gowns. Then came the bride on her father's arm.

Tracey was draped in floor-length white silk and a long, flowing white lace veil, carrying a matching sheaf of purple larkspurs over her arm.

On Roce's insistence they'd been picked fresh on Clayton property. He wore one pinned to the lapel of his tuxedo, as did his three brothers, who acted as Roce's best men. They stood near Tracey's aging minister, who would perform the ceremony.

All four of them wore Ralph Lauren midnight-blue, two-button tuxedos with black bow ties. As she clung to her wonderful father's arm and approached her husband-to-be, Roce's elegance took Tracey's breath away. His male beauty was unequaled. *I'm really going to marry him.*

Tracey's mother, looking lovely in a pale pink dress, sat in the front pew with Tracey's grandfather and her brother and his wife. Roce's family were in place in the front pew on the other side of the aisle. Alberta, beautifully dressed in an off-white silk suit, sat with Luis and Solana.

Except for Roce's father and her grandmother, everyone else they loved was here.

No detail had been overlooked for their midmorning church wedding. The reception would follow at Tracey's family home. Afterward, she and Roce would leave for the airport in Missoula. Once they returned from Greece, there would be another reception held at the Clayton ranch house for friends in that area of Montana.

Another step closer and Roce's hazel eyes locked on to hers. They gleamed like the gems brought out of the Sapphire Mountains. The moment they'd been waiting for had come. Her blood sang in her veins and she prayed she wouldn't collapse from too much joy.

The minister smiled at Tracey. "If you'll grasp your fiancé's hand, we'll begin." She passed her flowers to her mother, then took her place at Roce's side. He threaded his fingers through hers like he'd done so many times.

"This is it, sweetheart," he whispered.

Her heart was thumping so hard, she feared everyone in the chapel could hear it.

"There's no greater privilege for me than to marry Tracey to her beloved. I blessed her when she was brought into this world. I've watched her grow up from a sweet little girl into a lovely woman who has always been a blessing to her parents and family. I've lived long enough to hear her heartaches on occasion, and then rejoice to learn she's found the man of her dreams.

"Roce? I haven't had the privilege of knowing you. But when Tracey and I talked and she told me about you in the kind of glowing terms a man would give anything to hear from the woman he was going to marry, I knew this was going to be a very special, unique love match.

"Few people here know how you two met. It's worth mentioning that Tracey, a great horsewoman, discovered a horse in trouble, and through means I'm convinced came from above, Dr. Clayton was there to take care of it. I found their story inspiring, which is why I'm honored to perform their ceremony on this red-letter day.

"Do you, Dr. Rocelin Clayton, take Tracey Marcroft to be your lawfully wedded wife, to keep her in sickness and in health, to laugh with her, cry with her, build your life with this sweet woman, to love her, honor her and cherish her as God intended, all the days of your life?"

"I do."

The emotion in Roce's voice reached Tracey's heart.

The minister smiled at her. "I already know your answer, but so that your husband can hear it, do you, Tracey Marcroft, take Dr. Rocelin Clayton to be your lawfully wedded husband, to be his comfort, to support him in his care of God's creatures, to love him and only him, to be a light for him when things look dark, to be his delight no matter the season, to make your home a place he will always yearn for?"

Tracey looked into Roce's eyes. His love shone through with a luster she'd never seen before. "I will."

"Then by the power invested in me, I now pronounce you man and wife. I believe you have tokens to exchange."

She'd kept the simple gold wedding band for him in her left palm. Tracey had bought it secretly from Alberta, and now slid it on his ring finger. He in turn had a thin gold wedding band he placed on her finger next to the sapphire.

"What God has joined together, let no man put asunder. You may now kiss your bride."

"Darling," she whispered against his mouth, before he gave her a husband's kiss, hot with desire, lighting her on fire. She clung to him, forgetting they had an audience. They'd waited for this for so long.

Roce was the one who came to his senses first and relinquished her lips. The fire she glimpsed in his eyes excited her to the very core of her body. How were they going to last the twenty hours they'd be in flight from Missoula to Mykonos before they could be truly alone? But at least they would be together. *Forever.*

Mykonos, Greece

THE SHORT TAXI ride from Mykonos airport to the beach resort was the longest Roce had ever known. They could have stayed in New York overnight and then flown to Greece. But both of them wanted to spend all their time on the Aegean.

They were almost there. How was it possible to be so exhausted, yet trembling in desperation to be alone in order to begin their life as man and wife?

"Oh, look, Roce. How beautiful!" The sun had just dipped below the dark blue water when they arrived at their destination. The famous white Cycladic architecture flowing through a labyrinth of streets and white rocks didn't seem real.

Roce paid the driver, then they went inside the office of the building where they'd be staying and were promptly shown to their beach apartment with its colorful wooden balcony and stone floors. It was built right on the sand, with a small pool to bathe in. Beyond it was the sea as far as the eye could see.

The man put their bags down and kept talking until Roce told him they were on their honeymoon. Hearing those words, he left so fast Tracey started to laugh. "I need a quick shower," she said.

"Did you mean it when you promised to be my comfort?"

"Wait a minute and you'll find out."

She soon emerged from the bathroom wrapped in a white terry cloth guest bathrobe. He almost had a heart attack. "The bathroom is yours." Her smile lit up his universe.

Roce took a shower in record time and came out wearing his own robe. The room was dark except for the soft glow of the outside lights through the double doors opening on to the balcony.

Roce found his wife turning down the covers of the bed. She lifted her silvery-gold head as he walked toward her. "We're official now, Tracey. I've been waiting for this moment for so long, I'm trembling."

"So am I."

"I love you. Let me show you how much." He drew her into his arms and pulled her down on the bed with him. The second he covered her mouth with his own, their passion ignited. He'd never known such overpowering desire. The wonder of it all was that they didn't have to hold back, not ever again.

For the rest of the night they gave each other indescribable pleasure. His generous, loving wife thrilled him in ways he didn't know were possible. "You're so beautiful, so wonderful. What if we'd never met?" he whispered softly against her neck.

"I don't even want think about it, Roce. I didn't know love could be like this. Keep loving me, darling. Never let me go."

"As if I would."

Throughout the night, their hunger for each other knew no bounds. It was almost noon of the next day when he awakened first. Intoxicated by his brand-new wife's sweet scent and the sight of her lying next to him with her hair seductively disheveled, he studied her until he couldn't resist kissing her awake.

As she came alive, he moved her on top of him and they began the process of loving all over again. Sometime later, she raised herself up on one elbow and looked down at him. "You're so handsome it hurts, and I could stay like this forever. But I just noticed the time, and I know you've got to be hungry. All I have to do is pick up the phone and ask them to bring us some food."

He traced the line of her mouth. "Do it, but don't go away from me."

She rolled on her side to make the call. The second she hung up, he pulled her back to him. "When they knock, I'll get it."

"I'm not sure I can let you go for that long."

Roce was full of so much emotion, he crushed her in his arms. He kissed her succulent mouth over and over until they heard a knock. After sliding out from the covers, he threw on his robe and took some bills from his wallet to pay room service.

This time *he* was the one to put their tray in the middle of the bed. It reminded him of the night she'd helped him to bed after their ordeal in the mountains. Tracey lay propped on her side waiting for him.

Before joining her, he reached in his suitcase for the envelope Wymon had given him in the barn during his bachelor party. Then he walked back to the bed with it and stretched out on the other side of the tray.

He'd never tire of taking in her beauty. "You have no idea how alluring you look this morning."

Tracey beamed. "I could say the same thing about you. I adore you and your irresistible five o'clock shadow."

"I gave you a rash, but I'm not sorry."

"Neither am I," she said breathlessly. "What's in that envelope?"

"I'll tell you as soon as we've eaten our breakfast. This looks delicious."

When they'd finished, he put the tray on the floor at the side of the bed. "Now. Come over here and we'll look at this together."

She cuddled up to him while he opened the envelope and held up the map with the big red circle in the bottom left corner. "This, my love, represents the Clayton property."

Tracey sat up straighter. "Then that's the circle around your house."

He laughed long and hard. "Our house is in one portion of it. That circle is the outline of the property I now own." He reached in pull out the deed. "For our wedding present from the family, we've been given enough land to do whatever we want."

"Roce..."

"Fantastic, isn't it? My family expects we'll build a big ranch house, and kennels for the surgery. The list goes on and on, including a barn for our horses."

"It *is* fantastic. That's because they love you so much. But I have to tell you I love our little house in the big woods."

"So do I." He pulled her back into his arms. "But when the babies come, we're going to need more room."

"Babies—your babies. I can't wait. Can't you see our little boy or girl toddling around, with Daisy running circles because she's so excited?"

"All in good time, sweetheart. For a little while I just want you to myself."

She kissed the side of his mouth. "How little is a little while?"

Deep laughter rumbled out of him. "Are you telling me you want a baby right away?"

"Not if it isn't what you want."

He leaned over her. "If you want to know the truth, I'd love to start a family right now."

"You would?" She sounded ecstatic. "Oh, I love you, I love you. Let's not go anywhere for a while. Let's just stay in this little apartment."

"You're quite shameless. I hadn't realized."

"There's a lot you don't know about me, Dr. Clayton."

"I'm beginning to realize that, Mrs. Clayton. By

now you have to realize I'd do anything for you. All my life I've heard the expression 'getting your heart's desire.' I never dreamed it would actually happen to me."

"Thank heaven I drove by your house that day and found mine. Don't ever let me go, Roce."

"That works both ways, sweetheart. Now no more talk," he whispered against her lips before devouring her.

* * * * *

*Toly's story is next! Read more of
Rebecca Winters's*
SAPPHIRE MOUNTAIN COWBOYS *miniseries
in* ROPING HER CHRISTMAS COWBOY,
*coming December 2017,
only from Harlequin Western Romance!*

Get 2 Free Books,
Plus 2 Free Gifts—
just for trying the
Reader Service!

◆ HARLEQUIN®
Western Romance

By the time her mom rang the bell signaling lunch was
ready, Sloane had learned that Jason was from Idaho, he'd
been competing as a professional since he was eighteen and
he'd had six broken bones thanks to his career choice.

"Are you eating with us?" Phoebe asked as she slipped
her little hand into Jason's.

He smiled down at her. "I don't think they planned for the
extra mouth to feed."

Sloane huffed at that. "You've never met my mother and
her penchant for making twice as much food as needed."

"Please," Phoebe said.

"Well, how can I say no to such a nice invitation?"

Phoebe gave him a huge smile and shot off toward the
picnic area.

Jason chuckled. "Sweet kids."

"Yeah. And resilient."

He gave her a questioning look.

"They come from tough backgrounds. All of them have
had to face more than they should at their age."

"That's sad."

"It is. They seem to like you, though."

"And that annoys you."

"I didn't say that."

"You didn't have to." He grinned at her as he grabbed a ham-and-cheese sandwich and a couple of her mom's homemade oatmeal cookies.

"Sorry. I just don't know you, and these kids' safety is my responsibility."

"So this has nothing to do with the fact your sister is trying to set us up?"

"Well, there goes my hope that it was obvious only to me."

"It's not a bad idea. I'm a decent guy."

"Perhaps you are, but you're also going to be long gone by tomorrow night."

He nodded. "Fair enough."

Well, that reaction was unexpected. She'd thought he might try to encourage her to live a little, have some harmless fun. She wasn't a fuddy-duddy, but she also wasn't hot on the idea of being with a guy who'd no doubt been with several women before her and would be with several afterward.

Of course, she often doubted a serious relationship was for her either. She'd seen at a young age what loving someone too much could do to a person. The one time she'd believed she might have a future with a guy, she'd been proved wrong in a way that still stung years later.

Don't miss HER TEXAS RODEO COWBOY
by Trish Milburn, available September 2017
wherever Harlequin® Western Romance
books and ebooks are sold.

www.Harlequin.com

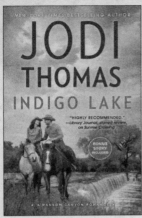

Earn points from all your Harlequin book purchases from wherever you shop.

Turn your points into *FREE BOOKS* of your choice
OR
EXCLUSIVE GIFTS from your favorite authors or series.

Join for FREE today at
www.HarlequinMyRewards.com.

Harlequin My Rewards is a free program (no fees) without any commitments or obligations.

MYR17